Ann-Marie was spooning off her favorite part of the banana split, the whipped cream and nuts, when she suddenly became conscious that a huge boy was sitting down next to her.

"Ann?" said the boy.

Startled, she looked at him, and her spoon slid to the floor. Biff Robertson! It was perfectly possible, Ann-Marie thought, that she might faint.

"Did I scare you or something?" Biff asked, his uncertain smile a little lopsided.

Ann-Marie gulped. "N-no," she said. "H-how did you know my name?"

Biff looked embarrassed. "Well, Ron told me what you look like. He said you'd be sitting here at the bar in that Mumford Athletic Department T-shirt, and a minute ago I came in and, well, uh, there you were."

Ron? She didn't know any Ron. Mumford Athletic Department T-shirt? Oh, no—Biff Robertson thought she was Ann Brierly!

Books by Janice Harrell

Puppy Love
Heavens to Bitsy
Secrets in the Garden
Killebrew's Daughter
Sugar 'n' Spice
Blue Skies and Lollipops
Birds of a Feather
With Love from Rome
Castles in Spain
A Risky Business
Starring Susy
They're Rioting in Room 32
Love and Pizza to Go
B.J. on Her Own
Masquerade

JANICE HARRELL earned her M.A. and Ph.D. from the University of Florida, and for a number of years taught English on the college level. She is the author of a number of books for teens, as well as a mystery novel for adults. She lives in North Carolina.

JANICE HARRELL

Masquerade

Keepsake
FROM
CROSSWINDS

CROSSWINDS
New York • Toronto • Sydney
Auckland • Manila

First publication August 1988

ISBN 0-373-88029-4

Dear Reader:

Welcome to our line of teen romances, Keepsake from Crosswinds. Here, as you can see, the focus is on the relationship between girls and boys, while the setting, story and the characters themselves contribute the variety and excitement you demand.

We hope that you are also enjoying our other novels under the Crosswinds logo. These lively stories feature young characters in contemporary situations.

As always, your comments and suggestions are welcome. They help us to keep Crosswinds where it belongs—at the very top of your reading list!

Nancy Jackson

Senior Editor
CROSSWINDS

Chapter One

If there was one person in the world that Ann-Marie Echersley couldn't stand it was Ann Brierly. Why did they have to have the same name? It had been bad enough sharing a table desk in the third grade. All year Miss Thomas had kept slamming a yardstick down on the table, trying to keep Ann B. in line. Unfortunately it was not Ann B., but her deskmate, Ann-Marie, who had spent the year shivering in a permanent state of nervousness.

Ever since then, Ann-Marie had tried to avoid Ann B. but it wasn't easy. The teachers' habit of placing well-behaved students next to known monsters was one of the problems. Another problem was that the Brierlys lived right next door to the Echersleys. It was awfully hard to ignore someone who was living right next door. To top it off, Ann B. was notorious. No matter how well Ann-Marie succeeded in keeping away from her, she still ended up having to listen to all the gossip about her.

For example, only weeks before school was out for the summer, the kids sitting at the bar of Lazlo's Ice Cream Parlor had watched through Lazlo's big glass window while Ann B. struck up an acquaintance with a man who was pushing a purple bicycle down the sidewalk. The man was wearing jeans and a black turtleneck and his thin, white face featured a full beard. Shortly afterward, Ann had sent her parents a picture postcard of downtown Juneau with a note scribbled on the back informing them that she was now homesteading in Alaska. Mr. Brierly had to have his brother come and look out for the hardware store while he flew up to Alaska to retrieve his daughter. It developed that the bearded man, who had only recently left the monastery, had little experience with women. That must have been why he had believed Ann B. when she told him she was a twenty-two-year old divorcée named Desirée who had always wanted to go homesteading in Alaska.

But the Alaska incident was only the most spectacular of a long list of Ann B.'s misadventures. In the second grade she had liberated the class ants from the ant farm, causing a full-scale panic among the second graders, whose lunchtime sandwiches were stored in the cloakroom. In the sixth grade she had got caught selling copies of the test on the Constitution. In the seventh grade she had brought a tube of Super Glue to school and after lunch Mrs. DeSantis had discovered that everything on her desk, from the box of paper clips to the stack of themes on "My Summer Vacation," had become permanently cemented to it. The fire department had to be summoned to unstick the class turtle from his rock.

Ann B.'s school record boasted numerous demerits. It was a mystery why she hadn't been permanently expelled. Some muttered darkly that it had to do with her father's being on the school board and the Governor's Task Force on Education. Others held with the theory that the principal, Mrs. Otto, believed it was the mission of the school to help girls like Ann B. When Ann-Marie gave up on the hope of Ann B.'s being expelled, in self-defense she developed the habit of pretending Ann B. didn't exist. She merely smiled vaguely in her direction and looked right past her. Presto-zippo—no Ann B. Ann-Marie had a very good imagination.

When Ann B. was brought back in disgrace from Alaska, however, Ann-Marie found herself behind her in the water fountain line and suddenly curiosity got the better of her.

"Did you like it in Alaska?" Ann-Marie asked, hating herself for showing the slightest interest.

Ann B. took a mirror out of her hip pocket and checked her lipstick. Finally she shrugged. "It was all right," she said. "Sorta cold."

"I guess you were sorry to leave," Ann-Marie suggested.

The other girl gave the matter serious thought as she hiked up her pants in back. "Nah," she replied. "It wasn't working out."

Ann-Marie awaited further details with rapt attention.

Ann B. explained, "He was always out chopping wood."

"Chopping wood?" Ann-Marie repeated faintly.

Ann B. shrugged. "He kept saying we were going to need it for the winter."

Just then Ann B. bent over the water fountain and turned the water on so carelessly that a spurt of water shot out to drench her bangs and spatter on her red socks. She straightened up laughing, beads of water glistening on her nose and in her eyebrows. Her Mumford Athletic Department T-shirt stretched as she caught her breath. All the boys in the hallway turned to look at her, for it was one of life's many injustices, thought Ann-Marie, that Ann B., with her moon-shaped face, her full dark eyebrows, her impossible raspberry-colored lipstick, and her funky clothes was attractive to boys.

At lunchtime, Ann-Marie continued to puzzle over the problem of Ann Brierly while she tore open her milk carton. "I truly don't understand why boys like her," she told her friend Felicia. "It doesn't make sense. Do *you* understand it?"

"Don't look at me like that," said Felicia.

"Like what?"

"Like Bambi," Felicia grumbled, stuffing a french fry in her mouth. "It's those eyes of yours. You're like those pictures in magazines that say Save This Child. Honestly, you ought to wear sunglasses. Look, Ann-Marie, I understand what you're saying. She gets a lot of attention from boys. It's a fact. Now, I've been giving it some thought and I think I've figured out why the boys like her. She's relaxed"

"Oh, she's *relaxed*, all right," Ann-Marie said darkly.

Felicia ticked off the points on her fingers. "She's friendly—"

"She's *friendly*, all right," said Ann-Marie.

"Would you please quit repeating what I'm saying. It makes me feel like I'm yelling into a canyon," complained Felicia. "Also she's got a terrific figure and she's always ready to do something crazy. That, in short, is why boys like her."

"But seriously, Felicia," said Ann-Marie, "don't you think there's something wrong with her? You should have heard her talking about that business of going to Alaska. 'It wasn't working out,' she said to me. A four-year-old could have seen it wasn't going to work out. But not her. The girl has zero brain."

"Oh, you're right. No question. There's nothing there. She's a total Twinkie, but the thing is, we can learn from her."

"You want us to become criminals?"

"No, dummy. I mean, we should pick up on the things that make her attractive and use them. Forget the criminal parts."

Ann-Marie did not give Felicia's suggestion her full attention. She had more important things on her mind. She was already busy unfolding the school newspaper. "Look at this," she said breathlessly. She folded the paper back to the sports section to show Felicia the headline that read Northern Knights Help with Special Olympics. The accompanying photograph of two hefty boys bending over a child in a wheelchair was captioned "Pictured are Mark Howe of Northern and Biff Robertson of FHS with Special Olympics participant Mikie Pringle."

Felicia eyed the photograph. "Awful picture of Mark," she said. "Funny how they always seem to catch you with your mouth open, isn't it?"

"I'm not talking about Mark," said Ann-Marie. "The other one. Biff."

"Cute," commented Felicia.

"Cute? Try gorgeous. Also, compassionate, loving, tender human being."

"I didn't know you knew this guy Biff."

"I don't know him," Ann-Marie said, thumping the newspaper down on the empty seat beside her. "How could I know him? He goes to FHS. But I have been watching him and I have decided he is my ideal."

"Maybe you could figure out a way to meet him."

"He doesn't even know I'm alive!" cried Ann-Marie. "I've been going to the Y's soccer games just to sort of look at him from afar, you know?" She wadded up her napkin and muttered, "If I were Ann B., I'd probably knock on his door, say I'd come to fix the air-conditioning and hang around until I got his parents to adopt me." She heaped her napkin and milk carton on top of her half-eaten hamburger, leaned her chin on her hand and regarded the stack of trash with despair.

That afternoon, she spotted Ann B. and Mark Howe standing near the ground floor lockers. Mark must know Biff Robertson, Ann-Marie thought. They worked together on the Special Olympics, after all. I could ask him to introduce me, maybe. Just then, Mark and Ann B. burst into raucous laughter. No, I couldn't do that, Ann-Marie decided suddenly. If Mark knew she had this thing about Biff Robertson he might go around telling everybody and she would die, just die.

She did not understand how Ann B. could be always laughing when life was so full of difficulties. It must be because of this business of her having zero brain, she decided.

When Ann-Marie got home from school, her sister, Susannah, was already home because the junior high let out a quarter of an hour earlier. Susannah was perched on the edge of a chair in the living room, practicing her flute.

"It's not fair," Ann-Marie said. She threw herself on the sofa and kicked off her shoes. "Why should all the boys like Ann B.? She's not pretty. She's not even nice. And on top of it she's dishonest!"

"She's staying with us the next few days," said Susannah. Raising her flute once more to her lips, she began a chromatic scale.

Ann-Marie stared at her in disbelief. "Mother!" she shrieked. She finally found her mother in the garage standing before a shower of sparks, welding some small pieces of rough iron. Mrs. Echersley was a small, slender woman with a strong resemblance to Pocahontas. Her skin was brown and her straight black hair was long enough to sit on. Today her hair was pulled together at the nape of her neck with a rubber band, and she was wearing a businesslike set of safety goggles. She pulled them off and turned around when she heard Ann-Marie.

"Hello, dear," she said. "Look, would you stand over there and tell me if you sense texture?"

Ann-Marie stood over next to where the garden rakes and hoes were hung and squinted at the iron pieces. "Lots of texture," she confirmed.

"Good." Mrs. Echersley prodded the iron scraps with her blowtorch. "I want it to suggest feathers from that angle."

"Mom, what's this about Ann B. coming to stay with us?"

Mrs. Echersley laid her blowtorch and safety goggles down on the Ping-Pong table. "I'd better take a break," she said. "I've been working on this thing so long I'm about to pass out."

"What about Ann B.?" Ann-Marie reminded her.

Mrs. Echersley was peeling off her gloves. "Poor Charles Brierly had a heart attack this morning. He's in a Chicago hospital and Martha had to fly up there to be with him. She called me from the hospital and asked me if we could look out for Ann for a few days until Charles's sister could get down here to help out. What could I say?"

"Why can't Ann look out after herself?" Ann-Marie wailed. "Why us?"

Mrs. Echersley, now moving back into the house, didn't bother to answer. It was all too obvious that while another sixteen-year-old might be left on her own for a few days, Ann Brierly needed strict supervision.

"She should be here any minute," Mrs. Echersley went on. "Mrs. Otto was going to break the news to her and drive her over to our house after school. I know you don't like her, dear, but keep in mind that she may be worried about her father and try to consider her feelings."

Ann-Marie was not sure Ann B. had feelings.

"We'll put a sleeping bag in your room," said her mother.

A quarter of an hour later, Ann B. showed up on the Echersleys' doorstep carrying an overnight bag. Mrs. Otto gave them all a cheerful wave as she left. Enviously Ann-Marie watched her drive away.

"Oh, you've got your things, Ann," Mrs. Echersley said. "Good."

"Mrs. Otto helped me pack," said Ann B., looking around.

That means Mrs. Otto was afraid to leave her alone even for a minute, Ann-Marie translated silently.

"Your mother tells me that your father is resting comfortably and there's no immediate cause for worry," said Mrs. Echersley.

"Mrs. Otto told me," said Ann B., her eyes shifting from one of Mrs. Echersley's colorful wall hangings to the pots of fresh basil in the living room bay window. Ann-Marie decided she was probably hoping the basil plants were illegal drugs.

"You can put your things back here in my room," said Ann-Marie. As she led Ann B. down the hall, she promised herself that she would keep a sharp eye on this girl every single minute. She wished she had looked her room over to make sure there was nothing lying around that could be easily pilfered.

Ann B.'s head turned as she looked around the bedroom, taking in the frilled white eyelet bedspread and the stuffed animals. She dropped her overnight case on the floor next to one of the tall stacks of library books. Her eyes rested on a large wall poster of a sheepdog with long bangs falling over his eyes. I See Best With My Heart, it said. A scornful smile began to grow on her lips.

"I like sheepdogs," said Ann-Marie defensively. "There's the sleeping bag you can use tonight." She pointed out the L. L. Bean sleeping bag that was rolled up under the shelves that held her stuffed animals.

Ann Brierly stuck a large pink square of bubble gum into her mouth and began chewing. "You better take the sleeping bag," she said. "I've got a bad back."

"I thought sleeping on the floor was good for bad backs," said Ann-Marie.

"Not for my kind of bad back. I hafta have a soft bed."

Ann-Marie gritted her teeth and reminded herself of her mother's admonition to consider Ann B.'s supposed feelings. She comforted herself as best she could with the thought that the arrangement would be only for a few nights.

Ann B. strolled over to the double closet and pulled the sliding doors open. Slowly she began leafing through the clothes in the closet.

"What are you doing?" Ann-Marie asked.

"Seeing what you've got," said Ann B. "If you've got anything I like, maybe we could trade."

"I won't have anything you like." Since Ann-Marie's taste ran to the understated and classic while Ann Brierly's taste tended toward the bag lady school of fashion, Ann-Marie felt she could be pretty sure of that.

Ann B. pulled out a white blouse with a pleated front and a Peter Pan collar. "I'd trade you something for this one," she said.

"That?" Ann-Marie said, astonished. "What would you do with something like that?"

"Use it for a disguise," suggested Ann B. She blew a large pink bubble.

Ann-Marie firmly took the blouse out of Ann B.'s hands, hung it back up in the closet and closed the doors. "I don't trade my clothes," she said. "My parents wouldn't like it."

During the three days Ann Brierly stayed with the Echersleys, Ann-Marie had a particularly horrible, though irrational, fear that Ann B. would steal one of her favorite stuffed animals. Maybe Baby Eyedy, the worn plush alligator Ann-Marie had had since she was two. Or Finkle, the faded basset hound she always slept with when she was away at camp. The thought preyed on her mind so much that she asked her mother to take all the stuffed animals off the shelf while the girls were at school and hide them under Susannah's bed. Mrs. Echersley immediately did what her daughter asked without asking any questions, which said something about the impact Ann B. was having on the household.

To everyone's relief, Ann Brierly's aunt arrived on Friday to take charge next door, and Ann packed up her overnight bag and went back where she belonged.

When Ann-Marie returned from her piano lesson that afternoon and found Ann B. gone, she had a very unpleasant feeling she couldn't quite pin down. She dashed into Susannah's room and began pulling out the stuffed animals hidden under the bed. A quick head count showed that none was missing.

Still feeling uneasy, Ann-Marie returned to her room. A crumpled T-shirt lay in front of her closet. She held it up and examined it. Mumford Athletic Department, it read. Dropping it, she flung the closet doors open and began going through her clothes. The white pleated blouse with the Peter Pan collar was missing. Also gone were her green-flowered wraparound skirt and a pair of red knickers. It could have been worse. At least she had never liked the knickers.

Chapter Two

FHS let out for the summer several days earlier than Northern, so while Ann-Marie was noting the losses from her wardrobe, Biff Robertson, already finished with school for the year, was watching his best friend pack a duffel bag for an Outward Bound program in Colorado.

Biff was a large boy with broad shoulders and muscular thighs. He moved slowly and carefully, as if he were afraid he was going to break something, a reasonable fear in view of his size. Although his rumpled hair was black, his eyes were blue and there were a few freckles across his nose.

His friend, Ron, currently busy stuffing a boot in his bag, was several inches shorter than Biff and sixty pounds lighter. Ron's every movement telegraphed an impression of nervous energy. In the fourth grade the two friends had been the same size, but looking at them now, that was hard to believe.

"I want you to keep an eye on Ann for me," Ron said.

"Your crazy girlfriend?" Biff asked, draping his leg over an arm of his chair.

"Have it your way. But she's not crazy."

Biff blushed a little, remembering the rumors he had heard about Ann Brierly running away to Alaska with some guy. He wondered if he should bring up this little matter to Ron. Better not, he decided. Nobody wants to hear that kind of stuff about a girl he likes.

"I know what you're thinking," said Ron. "And you can forget it. There was nothing to all that. She doesn't get along with her parents. She'll do anything to get away from home, that's all. Well, okay, maybe she's a little impulsive, and she does sometimes drink more than's good for her. I admit that. But she's working on it. And if you're thinking about that stolen car, hey, that was all a mix-up. You'll notice the guy never did press charges." Ron began rooting around in his dresser drawer, throwing socks out onto the floor, but then suddenly paused and looked at Biff with anxious eyes. "I'm worried, Biff. I think she may get in some real trouble if somebody doesn't keep an eye on her." He began scooping the socks up off the floor and tossing them on top of the bag. "You know the Vinson brothers?"

"Spike and Boomer? Sure. I mean, I don't exactly know them, but I know who you're talking about." Spike and Boomer had once attended FHS. An incident of breaking and entering had interrupted their education, landing them in Springfield Youth Center, a correctional facility for juveniles, and they hadn't bothered to finish high school when they returned.

"Well, Ann and I were in Dino's splitting an order of fried onion rings, you know, and in came Spike and Boomer. I don't know how to put this, but I had the feeling there was something funny going on. You know how I get these feelings? I promise you, it just seemed like they were up to something."

"So what? Who cares what they're up to?"

"When I'd look at one of them, it was like they were always just looking away. Like they didn't want me to catch them looking at us. And Ann was acting sort of funny, you know? Antsy. I tell you, I wouldn't put it past those two to get her mixed up in something that's not legal. Using her for a patsy somehow or other. Maybe they've already started trying to rope her into something. If I could hang around here a while longer, I'm sure I could get her to tell me about it, but here I've got to take off tomorrow morning.''

Biff didn't believe for a minute that Ron's girl was an innocent victim type. He had never met her, but he had heard enough about her to know she was nothing but trouble. Ron was too trusting, that was his problem.

Biff avoided Ron's eyes by studying his thumbnail, which had gotten badly blackened when one of his weights fell on it.

''Look, Biff, have I ever asked you to do anything for me before?''

''Sure,'' Biff said.

''Nothing big, anyway,'' Ron interjected quickly. ''All I'm asking is that you keep an eye on her. Maybe this junk is all my imagination, huh? But if it's not, you can keep those jerks away from her. They're not going to mess with you.''

''How do you figure I could keep an eye on her, exactly, huh? I don't even know her.''

''Easy. Go into Lazlo's just about any afternoon and she'll be there. I'd tell you to call her up, but her parents are so weird about letting her talk to guys you probably couldn't even get through. Look, if you see her in Lazlo's, you'll recognize her right off. She's beautiful. And she'll be sitting right up there at the bar, probably wearing one of those Mumford Athletic Department T-shirts. She loves those things. She must have a zillion of them. She's a big Eddie Murphy fan. Just go over, tell her who you are and say you're a friend of mine. No problem. Her parents aren't so crazy about her going out with guys, but you can probably fix it up to meet her at Lazlo's and go somewhere to talk. Take her to a movie or something. Try and find out what's going on.''

"Look, she's a big girl, Ron. She can take care of herself.''

"Remember when we became blood brothers?''

"For Pete's sake, we were seven years old. Don't remind me.''

"And we swore to defend each other against all the perils of land and sea and outer space?''

Biff smiled reluctantly.

"Well, Spike and Boomer are perils, I'm telling you. Just do this one thing for me, Biff, old buddy.''

Afterward, Biff could not quite understand how Ron had gotten him to agree to his crazy plan. He suspected the turning point had been when Ron pointed out that if he was swept away in white water somewhere in Colorado Biff was going to be darn sorry he hadn't granted his best friend's final request.

Ron's last word on the subject of Ann had been called out as he trotted toward his plane shortly after dawn the next morning. "Look but don't touch," he yelled to Biff. "Don't forget who she belongs to, huh?"

"What did he say?" said Ron's mother, raising her voice above the roar of the jet.

"Nothing," Biff yelled back at her.

"What's an 'ingenue'?" asked Susannah, looking up from *TV Week*. "It says here 'The admittedly talented Miss Devereaux is long past playing ingenue parts.'"

"It's a French word," her father explained, looking up from the invoices he was trying to organize. Mr. Echersley never passed up a chance to point out the derivation of a word. "Ingenue," he went on, "is the word used to describe the role of an innocent, unworldly young woman."

"An ingenue is someone who hasn't done anything," put in Ann-Marie. "An ingenue does her homework and practices her piano, but nobody ever notices her because she hasn't done anything worth talking about. Being an ingenue is like being a nonentity. It is absolutely the most boring kind of part an actress can play. I, for instance, am an ingenue.''

Ann-Marie's mother bent over and kissed the top of her head. ''I don't think you're a nonentity. I think you're a smart, dear, very special girl.''

''You're my mother,'' groaned Ann-Marie. ''I'd be in pretty bad shape if my own mother didn't think I was special.''

When the Y's spring soccer league had folded for the season, Ann-Marie's hopes of meeting Biff Robertson had vanished and as a result she was feeling unusually gloomy. As long as she had been hanging around the soccer fields, she could nourish pleasant fantasies. The soccer ball might be kicked out of bounds. It might even, with luck, knock her out. Farmingdale's forward, Biff Robertson, known for his sensitivity and kindness, might under these circumstances be so overcome with guilt that he would insist on riding with her to the hospital. She could imagine her eyes fluttering helplessly, then opening to see his concerned face. ''You're all right!'' he would exclaim, clasping her pale hand in his. It could well be the beginning of something beautiful.

Yes, that fantasy had a good deal to recommend it, not the least of which was that a soccer ball was pretty soft and Ann-Marie had the feeling it might not hurt too much to be knocked out by one.

"Nothing ever happens to me," Ann-Marie complained.

"You need something to do, that's all," said her mother. "What did Miss Simmons say about the library job?"

"She can only use me one morning a week," said Ann-Marie.

"I can always use help at the store," put in her father.

Ann-Marie pretended not to hear him. She hated working at her father's health food store. The only people who ever came in were aging hippies stocking up on herb tea and elderly people worried about their health. They were a depressing bunch. Arthritis, high cholesterol and osteoporosis were not the sorts of things she wanted to spend the summer discussing. The people Ann-Marie wanted to meet, namely kids her own age, hung around the fast-food joints, stuffing themselves with empty calories, fat and cholesterol. They generally enjoyed the best of health in spite of this, which sometimes made her wonder if health food was all it was cracked up to be. But getting a job at a fast-food place was hopeless. All those jobs were filled by kids who worked at them all year round and Ann-Marie's parents wouldn't allow her to work at a part-time job during the school year.

The phone rang and Ann-Marie's father, still intent on his invoices, grimaced, and picked it up. "Hello? Yes, she's right here." He held out the receiver. "Felicia for you."

"I'll take it in my room," Ann-Marie said.

She dashed back to her room, grabbed the phone off her bedside table and threw herself down on the bed. She was such a small person, the bed scarcely shuddered from the impact.

"Ann-Marie?" said Felicia. "I have been practicing meditation. It's a part of my three-point program, remember? I am going to have a more relaxed manner and this is the first step. Of course, being relaxed is easy around the house. What I want to do is to put my new relaxation techniques to the test. I'm going to go by Lazlo's this afternoon and get a table right back there by the video games where the guys hang out, and then see how relaxed I can be. Can you meet me at Lazlo's?"

"Won't it be a better test if you're there by yourself?"

"I said test," said Felicia, "not suicide. Of course, I don't want to go by myself. I'd take one look at all those guys and positively fall apart."

After she hung up, Ann-Marie spent a moment or two figuring out what to wear over to

Lazlo's. It's not that I don't know what the latest thing is, she thought, peering into her closet doubtfully. It was just that when it actually came to buying it, her nerve failed.

She couldn't understand why she was so timid about clothes. Her parents had been, in their time, very "with it" as people used to say in those days. She had seen a snapshot of her father with a peace sign peeping from below a huge, wiry beard. Her mother, standing barefoot beside him in a flower print smock and long earrings, had looked equally hip. Ann-Marie recalled that when she had described her parents as being "hippies" they had recoiled. "Bohemians," her father had corrected her. Ann-Marie hadn't argued. She figured she knew a hippie when she saw one. The problem was that the hip gene seemed to have skipped her entirely. She decided she must be some throwback to the fifties or something.

Flipping through her closet, her eye fell on the T-shirt Ann B. had left behind. It had been sent to the laundry with the rest of the shirts and now hung on a hanger, washed and neatly ironed. She took it down and looked at it. Well, why not? This is just the sort of thing people wear to Lazlo's. She slipped out of her frayed shorts and put on the T-shirt and some tapered jeans slit up the sides.

She reflected that unlike Felicia, she had no difficulty at all being relaxed at Lazlo's. She didn't go there very often, not being overly fond either of ice cream or of hanging around, but when she did go, she was never nervous because she was sure no one would pay any attention to her. With her soft brown hair, which swung just a few inches lower than her ears, her large brown eyes, and her conventional clothes she could, she thought, have been stuffed by a taxidermist and sent to the Smithsonian as a perfect example of late eighties nondescriptness. No one would ever notice her at Lazlo's. After all, no one ever had.

When she pulled up in front of the ice cream parlor in her mother's car, she noticed that the place did not look crowded. Saturday afternoons were evidently not a peak time in the summer. She pushed the heavy glass door open and looked around for Felicia. Some video-game addicts were in the back by the machines. "Aw riiight," one yelled as his machine exploded in a shower of colored lights and pinging noises. Ann-Marie suspected that it was going to be harder than Felicia thought to relax at a table back there next to the video machines. Personally she preferred a quieter part of the ice cream shop. Prepared to wait, she took a stool at the counter and ordered a banana split.

She was spooning off her favorite part, the whipped cream and nuts, when she suddenly became conscious that a huge boy was sitting down next to her. Her eyes rested on his large thighs, which stretched his Levi's to a point that fully tested the tensile strength of the denim. She stared at her spoon, afraid to look up.

"Ann?" said the boy.

Startled she looked at him and her spoon slid to the floor. Landing with a clatter, it splattered whipped cream along the base of the counter. Biff Robertson! It was perfectly possible, Ann-Marie thought, that she might faint. "Did I scare you or something?" Biff asked, his uncertain smile a little lopsided.

Ann-Marie gulped. "N-no," she said.

One thought was paramount in her mind—it was vitally important that she herself not slip to the floor like her spoon. To make sure she wouldn't, she clutched the edges of the stool with both hands. "H-how did you know my name?" she asked.

Biff looked embarrassed. "Well, Ron told me what you look like. He said you'd be sitting here at the bar in that Mumford Athletic Department T-shirt, and a minute ago, I came in and, well, uh, there you were."

Whoops of delight exploded back near the video games. Some quick electronic pings were followed by a ringing bell.

Ron? She didn't know any Ron. Mumford Athletic Department T-shirt? Oh, no—Biff Robertson thought she was Ann Brierly!

Ann-Marie struggled to restore her regular breathing pattern. "May I have another spoon, please?" she asked the man behind the counter. She could feel a pulse pounding in her temple and was amazed at how calm her voice sounded. The man put down the cloth with which he was silently wiping the bar and went to get her a spoon.

"You're going to think this sounds crazy," said Biff, "but Ron asked me to sort of watch out for you while he was gone. I told him it was a nutty idea, but you know Ron. You can't tell him anything." Biff couldn't stop looking at the girl beside him. He had to admit he was floored. She wasn't a bit what he'd expected. Knowing Ron's taste in girls, he hadn't paid much attention when Ron said she was beautiful. Ron was always getting carried away. But this girl had something, all right. Those big brown eyes rimmed with black lashes, the sort of soft, trembling lips and baby fine, shiny hair.

The soda jerk laid a spoon down beside Ann's banana split.

"Give me a chocolate shake and a large fries," said Biff. He was glad to have food to distract him for a minute because he realized he was going to have to get a grip on himself or he would be taken in by this Ann girl the way Ron had been, the poor sucker. He had to forcefully remind himself that this was the girl who had taken off to Alaska with a perfect stranger, that she had been involved in some funny business with a stolen car, and that she got drunk, which as far as Biff was concerned was the absolute ultimate turnoff.

Biff couldn't stop himself from sneaking glances at her. He tried to remember everything Ron had told him about her. The trouble was when Ron fell for a girl he went on and on about her and a fella tended to tune him out so the details were a bit foggy, but somehow Biff had expected a big, blowzy type, with a quick comeback. He saw now that he had it all wrong. He was going to have to feel his way carefully until he figured this one out. On the one hand, now that he had met Ann, he thought maybe Ron was right about her needing somebody to watch out for her. But on the other hand, he hadn't forgotten all the stuff he'd heard about her, either.

The soda jerk slammed the milk shake down on the counter in front of Biff. Biff looked at it a second as if surprised to see it there, then dug in a spoon and began to eat with determination.

It was at this point that Ann-Marie spotted Felicia pushing on the heavy glass door of Lazlo's. Felicia's eyes were half closed and when she stepped over the threshold, she raised a hand to cover her mouth as she yawned. Ann-Marie thought it looked as if Felicia were overdoing this relaxation bit. Relaxing is good, yes, but not sleepwalking. She shot Felicia a look full of pleading, but Felicia was so busy relaxing that at first she didn't see Ann-Marie. When she did, she took one startled look at Biff then turned around and exited the ice cream shop as quickly as if she had been in a revolving door. Ann-Marie breathed a small sigh of relief. She didn't see how she could concentrate on the current crisis if she had to worry about Felicia's three-point plan on top of everything else.

"You want to go to a movie tonight?" Biff asked abruptly.

"Uh, sure," said Ann-Marie, blinking rapidly. "That sounds good."

"You live out in Northgreen somewhere, don't you?"

"That's right—933 Wickerberry Lane. It's the white house, two blocks past Northgreen Baptist church, right where you turn off into the subdivision. Here." She jotted down her address and phone number on a napkin for him.

Biff's eyes flickered uneasily to her face. "Your folks won't mind if I come on by the house? I could meet you here if that would be better."

"Oh, they won't mind," said Ann-Marie. What they would mind, she thought as she took another bite of her melting ice cream, would be her sneaking around behind their backs to meet boys, which was evidently the practice of Ann B.

"You know, you're different from what I expected," said Biff, looking at her hard.

Ann-Marie smiled a little nervously and licked the chocolate off her spoon. "I am?"

"Yeah. Well, I guess it's tough to get an idea of what somebody's like just by hearing people talk about them."

"I guess so," Ann-Marie said. She couldn't believe she was doing this. She was an impostor. She was actually letting him go on thinking she was Ann B. The problem was that she could already imagine what would happen if she told him she was only Ann-Marie Echersley. "Oops! Sorry," he would say. Then he would pick up his milk shake and fries and walk out of her life. For good. She couldn't stand it. This was her chance, her only chance, to sit close to Biff Robertson and to feel her heart stop beating when he smiled at her. "You know, there's something familiar about you," Biff said. "It's like I've seen you before but I can't think where."

Ann-Marie felt hot color rushing to her face. "I'm a soccer fan," she said.

"That's it. I must have seen you at a game. Funny. I got the idea from Ron that you weren't into sports much."

"Just soccer," said Ann-Marie in a stifled voice. She pawed at her ice cream with her spoon.

"Well, Ron got off all right," he said. "I guess he told you he's really looking forward to climbing up those cliff faces, shooting the white water in a raft and all. Probably get himself killed." Ann's alarmed eyes lifted to Biff's face, and he felt a sudden painful jolt of sympathy. She must really like old Ron, he thought, feeling oddly let down. "I was just kidding," he assured her. "Ron can take care of himself. Don't worry about him." He pushed his tall glass away from him. "Well, I'll see you tonight then. Seven-thirtyish. Okay? Oh, my name is Biff Robertson."

She nodded mutely.

Biff imagined he could feel her gaze boring into his back as he walked away from the counter. When he got outside he turned around and looked back at her through the big glass windows. She was leaning on the counter, a frail little figure in a Mumford Athletic Department shirt, sitting with her hands buried in her hair. She looked as if she had just got some terrible news. He supposed he had given her a scare about Ron. As he walked away from Lazlo's, he wondered what in the name of heaven he had gotten himself into.

Chapter Three

You told him you were Ann Brierly!" screeched Felicia.

Ann-Marie winced. "Hush," she implored. "Mom and Dad are going to hear you." Felicia had been waiting for Ann-Marie at the house when she got back from Lazlo's, keen to hear how Ann-Marie had managed to meet the man of her dreams. She had not, however, been at all prepared for the truth.

"I can't believe you did that," whispered Felicia. "You must have been absolutely crackers. How could you *possibly* have told him you were Ann Brierly?"

"You don't think it was a good idea?"

Felicia silently rolled her eyes.

"No, listen, Felicia. I'm not sure it's such a bad idea. I mean, how is it different from wearing false eyelashes or a girdle? People do that sort of thing all the time. It sort of gets somebody's attention. It's not exactly the same thing as an actual lie."

Felicia fell back onto the bed and groaned. Finally, propping herself up on one elbow, she said, "You are an impostor. And you are not just an ordinary impostor, you are impersonating the wildest girl at Northern Nash, a girl whose reputation is so bad she is virtually a legend in her own time. And you say it's like wearing a *girdle*?" She fell back on the bed.

Ann-Marie looked anxious. "I didn't exactly tell him I was Ann B. I just didn't deny it, that's all."

Felicia groaned again.

Ann-Marie sat down on the bed beside Felicia. "You see," she said, "I knew if I told him he had the wrong girl, he would leave and I'd never see him again. You do understand that, don't you? That way, I *knew* I'd never see him again. This way, I at least have a chance. He's noticed me now. He's even asked me out, right? I can always tell him later that there's been a little mix-up."

"He hasn't asked you out, Ann-Marie. He has asked Ann B. out. And he's only doing that because he promised this friend of his he'd look out after dumb old Ann B. This is not a real date."

"It's a start, though. I can't get to know him if I never spend some time with him, can I? So, I'll spend a little time with him, and then when we know each other a little better, I'll explain everything."

"Hasn't it occurred to you that he's going to be mad when he finds out?" asked Felicia. She raised a finger. "Just remember 'Oh, what a tangled web we weave when first we practice to deceive.' And don't say I didn't warn you."

"Oh, it's not that bad," said Ann-Marie, hoping she was right.

When Biff drove by his grandparents' dignified two-story house, he was surprised to see two police cars outside. Alarmed, he pulled up in the driveway and ran inside.

"Gram?" he called. "Granddad?"

His grandmother came in the kitchen from the living room. Tears were making wet tracks down her cheeks.

"Is something wrong with Granddad?" he asked, fear squeezing his chest.

His grandmother laughed a little uncertainly. "No, no, darling, nothing like that. It's so silly, but I just can't stop crying. We've been burglarized. It makes a person feel so unsafe, somehow, but nobody's been hurt and that's the important thing.'' She blew her nose, then threw her arms around Biff's waist and hugged him. A small elegant woman with curly gray hair, she only came up to Biff's chin these days. ''But Granddad is naturally very upset.''

''What did they get?''

''The etchings, of course. Except for that, just Granddad's coin collection. But it's the etchings he's grieving over, poor thing. He's in talking to the police now.''

''Weren't they insured?''

''Oh, yes, though maybe not for their full value. But it's not the money your grandfather wants. He did love those things.'' She wiped her eyes. ''The police asked us who knew about them. We had to say all sorts of people knew. I'm afraid it may have been a mistake to let the museum borrow them for that exhibit. The fact is, anybody who could read the exhibit label would know we owned them. And there was an article about it in the local paper at the time.''

As long as Biff could remember, the two Rembrandt etchings had been hung in his grandparents' bedroom on the north wall where no sun would ever strike them. A fancy new central air system had been installed ten years ago to ensure their continued health and comfort. Biff's grandmother sometimes insisted she'd had a cold in the head ever since, but Biff's grandfather said it was all in her imagination. It was hard for Biff to believe that the etchings, which his grandfather had coddled and treasured all these many years, were actually gone.

"Oh, Lord," murmured Biff. "It is pretty bad, isn't it? Do the police think they can get them back?"

His grandmother made a hopeless gesture.

Biff heard the front door opening. "We'll be in touch, Judge," said a deep voice. "We'll let you know if we hear anything."

The front door closed and Biff's grandfather walked into the kitchen. He was a tall, imposing man with a thick mane of white hair. On either side of his nose began deeply grooved lines that bracketed his mouth, giving him the stern expression that had served him well in his judicial career. Biff was distressed to see that his grandfather's eyes were rimmed with pink. The old man sat down heavily at the kitchen table.

"What did they say?" asked Biff.

"They couldn't add anything to what the men told us this morning. No fingerprints, no leads. They've gotten in touch with a network in New York that specializes in art thefts, but from what they said, I could see there isn't much hope. In the past number of years, even some significant paintings have disappeared without a trace, and an etching isn't individual like a painting. A collector could buy a stolen one in all good faith, presumably. Well, this should be a lesson to me, Helen, about laying up my treasure on earth where thieves can break in."

Biff and his grandmother exchanged a glance. When his grandfather started quoting scripture there wasn't much you could do to cheer him up.

"There's no use sitting around here and moping," Judge Robertson said. "I think I'll take a walk." The vinyl floor protested as he scooted his chair back. "I don't expect those people from the burglar-alarm firm until tomorrow morning, but if they show up while I'm gone, tell them to come back later. I want to take a hand personally in the arrangements."

A moment later, Biff and his grandmother heard the clatter of Judge Robertson's cane in the hallway and then an explosion of wrathful curses as some umbrellas came tumbling out of the umbrella stand. Biff and Gram knew better than to speak as they heard the crashing sound of Judge Robertson kicking the umbrella stand. They sat quietly in the kitchen until they heard the front door slam.

"A burglar alarm?" asked Biff. "Isn't it kind of late for that?"

Gram wrung her hands. "You don't know what it's like, Biff. The house just doesn't seem safe anymore. It's a terrible feeling to think these people can just walk right in anytime they like."

"When did it happen?"

"Last night. We were in Raleigh attending the gala for the Friends of the Museum, and you know your grandfather doesn't see well enough to drive at night these days, so we stayed at a hotel."

"Who knew that you were going to stay over?"

"I just don't know. Of course, any number of people might have known. And as the police pointed out, anyone who was keeping an eye on the house would have been able to see that one of the cars was gone. That's what bothers me. Imagine somebody watching the house! We're going to get an unlisted number as soon as possible." Gram shivered.

"Do Mom and Dad know?"

"We talked to Phil and Alice a few minutes ago. It's just so hard to believe. Those etchings have been a part of this house for forty years and now they're gone! Every time I look at that empty place on the wall I get an awful feeling." She blew her nose. "I don't think they're going to recover them, Biff. I really don't."

He patted her hand. "You never can tell. Maybe we'll get lucky."

Biff was still thinking about the burglary that evening when he drove over to pick up Ann. He was afraid his grandfather was right. The etchings were gone for good. With something like a stereo, you figured there was always a hope the cops would catch the thieves with the goods. But this had probably been pulled by some big art theft ring from out of town. The whole thing was pretty depressing.

He pulled his car up into the driveway of 933 Wickerberry Lane and looked at the Colonial style house ahead of him with mild anxiety. After the billing Ann's parents had got from Ron he wasn't exactly dying to meet them. He hated it when a girl's parents looked at him as if he were an accredited kidnapper. Pushing his hands into his pockets, he made his way up the brick walkway and rang the bell.

The door opened almost at once and Biff found himself facing a barefoot woman who looked like an Indian. She seemed to have some sort of yarn woven into her long black braids. She was dressed in jeans and was wearing a heavy turquoise-and-silver ornament hung on a thong around her neck. "You must be Biff," she said. "Come in out of the heat."

He was still searching for some sort of clue about who she was as he followed her into the living room. Some dinky looking plants were growing in pots in the bay window, and Biff had to make his way carefully to avoid hitting the hanging baskets near the window.

Large oriental-looking cushions were stacked around the room for extra seating, but he was relieved to see there were some ordinary chairs, as well.

His attention was caught by an elaborate structure hanging on the wall behind the couch. It was decidedly three-dimensional, with stiff fabric stretched over twiggy branches that jutted out over the sofa. Its chief colors were tangerine and hot pink. A good many tiny little mirrors had been glued to it so that it glittered in places, and at the top was a spray of stiff black threads that looked like a giant eyelash.

Biff had been dragged into enough art museums by his grandparents not to be at all put off by the odd structure. Actually he kind of liked it.

A barefoot man in jeans had been lounging on a leather sofa under the artwork. He sat up and smiled when Biff came in. "Hey, man. You've got to be Biff."

"Yes, sir," said Biff, still mesmerized by the thing on the wall. "India," he said suddenly.

"It's like those Indian decorations you see sometimes."

"One of my wife's pieces," said Ann's dad proudly.

"My Frank Stella period," said the woman, tugging on a braid. She was sitting on one of the fat cushions, her legs folded yoga style under her. She gestured toward it. "Some people don't like the work to reach toward you, but what I always say is, the traditional canvas is dead. It's just not a viable alternative anymore. It's not my fault. We have to work where we are. We can't go backward." She had a gentle voice, rather like Ann's.

"Oh, right," Biff said. Then reminding himself with an effort that he was talking to a mother, he added a belated, "ma'am."

Ann appeared at the door of the living room in jeans and some kind of soft-looking shirt. Her earrings caught the light as she looked toward Biff. "I guess I'm ready," she said. She had a look in her eyes that Felicia would have instantly recognized as Save This Child. In spite of all Biff's many mental reservations, he felt his heart turn over.

By the time they had made it out to the car, Biff had it all figured out. Ann's parents seemed very nice, but anybody with half an eye could see they were hippies. Probably when she was out stealing cars and getting drunk they just figured she was finding herself or something. It was all very simple. Ann was a product of permissive-style upbringing he had heard about.

Chapter Four

Biff started the engine.

"I hope my parents didn't make you nervous," Ann said.

"I liked them." Biff looked at her, thinking that she was like her parents—soft-spoken and a little different.

"You should have come in your bare feet," she said. "My parents really feel *close* to anybody who's barefoot. They even feel close to people wearing sandals. We went to the Impressionists exhibit in D.C. last year and I lost track of Mom in the museum shop. When I found her she was sitting on a bench with this barefoot guy talking about the meaning of life. She didn't even *know* him. Not that I'm complaining. It could be worse. My parents have these good friends they've known since they were in college and do you know what their kids are named? Justice, he's the oldest; Charity, she's Susannah's age; and Third.''

''Third?''

''Third. Because he was the third child. Isn't that just terrible?''

''Ann is a nice name,'' he said.

For some reason, she began blushing. ''Yes,'' she agreed in a muffled voice.

When they got to the Cardinal Theater, Biff saw there was a line outside. That's good, he thought. Standing in the line would give them more time to talk and after all he was supposed to be drawing Ann out, finding out if she was mixed up in anything with Spike and Boomer. Maybe the movie wasn't such a hot idea when he came to think of it. Not much chance for talking in a movie. And when you came right down to it, you needed exactly the right atmosphere to work around to asking somebody if she were considering committing a felony.

Biff parked the car and they joined the line on the sidewalk. First thing, Biff checked around to see if anybody was in the line that he knew. The fact was he didn't want it to get back to his parents that he was going out with Ann. From experience Biff had learned that his father knew things about people all over town that were not to their credit. His dad was always passing the time of the day with the police out in the hallway of the courthouse, which probably accounted for it. That business of the stolen car was exactly the sort of thing his father might know about. And how he would feel about Biff getting mixed up with somebody who had stolen a car Biff hated to think.

He thrust his hands in his jeans pockets. "Nice weather we're having," he said.

"Oh, yes," Ann agreed, looking up at him. "Lovely."

Lovely is what you are, Biff thought suddenly, looking into her eyes. Then he blushed, deeply thankful that she could not read his mind.

The line had moved ahead without them and he put his hand at Ann's waist and guided her forward. He would have liked to put his arms around her and kiss her sweet little nose. He was obviously stark, staring nuts, he thought glumly. "Looks like we're going to miss the first part of it," he observed.

But the line began moving a little more quickly and a few minutes later they were in the lobby, sniffing the smell of buttered popcorn. There was a big crowd inside and as people churned toward the popcorn machine, Biff and Ann were pressed close up against each other.

"Let's forget the popcorn," Biff said desperately. He grabbed her hand and they fought their way through the crowd to the swinging doors of the theater. Stepping inside, in the darkness, he felt suddenly blind and disoriented, conscious only of Ann's hand, small and confiding in his. On the bright screen ahead a huge train steamed past roaring and wailing.

"Here are some seats," she whispered. "Unless this is too far back for you."

"No, that's okay," he said. They edged past a couple eating popcorn, and Biff collapsed onto one of the folding seats. The next time Ron wanted a favor, Biff swore to himself, he could forget it.

Ahead of them on the screen, a body thrown off the train was rolling down an embankment. As it stopped rolling, the camera focused close up on the knife in its back. Ann's mouth opened, and her face registered horror.

Biff leaned over and whispered in her ear, "I'll go back and get us some popcorn in a minute."

On-screen, the train's whistle shrieked just then and he wasn't even sure she had heard him. He hunched down in his seat and throughout the rest of the movie concentrated on wishing he were dead.

Later, when the movie was over, the mob started pouring out of the theater and Biff and Ann, carried along by the crowd, were talking so that for a minute Biff almost forgot he was with Ron's girl. "It just didn't make sense," she was saying, as they dodged a man carrying a crying toddler on his back. "When you think about it, if Eugene is supposed to be so rich and all, why did he go risking his life to steal the emeralds? Okay," she said, skipping down the curb, "so he thought he should have got the family emeralds just because he was the oldest son. He got everything else, didn't he? If he was so crazy for emeralds, he would have just bought himself some at Tiffany's or something. Do you see what I mean?"

"Nope. I say it makes sense. It's just human nature to want what you can't have." Having said that, he suddenly remembered whose girlfriend Ann was and opened the car door for her, standing stiffly by the door, as if he were a chauffeur.

Slamming the door shut, he walked around to the other side and slid in behind the wheel. "We never did get that popcorn," he said gloomily.

Gazing over at her he noticed a little mole in the tail of her eyebrow and the way little dimples appeared in her cheeks when she smiled. He thought she was the most adorable thing he had ever seen. He was even beginning to think that business about the stolen car had actually been some mix-up just the way Ron said.

"I got so caught up in the movie," she said, "I forgot all about the popcorn."

"We can drive by Wendy's and pick something up," he said. He set his lips in a firm line and turned on the ignition. He would feed the girl and take her home before his feelings got out of hand. "The drive-thru window," he added with decision.

"Okay," she said, looking at him a little anxiously.

They drove for a moment in silence. "How long is it you and Ron have been going together?" Biff asked.

She jumped when he spoke, then turned away from him to gaze out the window into the darkness. "Oh, I don't know," she said. "You know how it is."

"I guess when you fall for somebody it seems like you've known them forever," he said morosely.

She looked back over her shoulder and smiled briefly. He noticed that her hair was the sort of hair you'd like to run your fingers through. He cleared his throat.

"The thing is, Ron got this idea you had something on your mind," Biff said. "That's why he asked me to look you up. He figured maybe I could help out. He thought it might have something to do with Spike and Boomer Vinson.'' Since he had stopped at a traffic light, he was able to watch her reaction closely.

"Spike and Boomer!" she exclaimed. "Those juvenile delinquents—that is, well—I guess Ron must have gotten the wrong idea somehow.''

Biff reluctantly decided Ron was right about Ann being mixed up with those two. She was looking guilty, that was for sure. He'd never seen somebody look so guilty. He hoped she wasn't up to something so serious that it would get her three to five in prison. A sweet-looking girl like that—who would have believed she even knew the Vinsons? He sighed and drove a few blocks, then turned into Wendy's parking lot. "Look, Ann, you can trust me. Just pretend I'm Ron. I'm only standing in for him while he's out there. Why don't you just tell me what's going on?''

"Oh, I *do* trust you," she said earnestly.

Biff pulled up to the drive-thru speaker and a garbled electronic voice said, "Welcome to Wendy's. May I take your order, please?''

"What do you want?" Biff asked her.

"Uh, a large Pepsi, and would you like to split some fries, maybe?''

Biff turned back to the speaker and said gruffly, "A large Frosty, a large Pepsi and two large fries."

The electronic voice seemed to be expressing satisfaction with the order as Biff stepped on the gas and sped up to the take-out window. He figured it would be better not to share the fries. That was why he had ordered two. A smart move. He had the idea that reaching into the same bag like that, with his fingers and Ann's fingers touching, it could be hard to remain cool and impartial. He needed to keep his head straight.

After a few minutes, the glass door of the drive-in window slid open and an arm held out two paper bags to him. Biff took the bags, handed the drinks over to Ann and took the other bag himself. He fished out a few french fries, which he ate at once; then, putting the bag down by the gearshift, he stepped on the gas again. As he careened the car around the restaurant, Ann began getting the drinks out of the bag. Biff noticed that the tops didn't seem to have been secured properly. It drove him crazy the way the simplest order from these fast-food places came with enough plastic, paper, napkins, bags and straws to junk up the whole car, but he wasn't in any shape to be choosy. Time was of the essence. He needed to extract Ann's

secret from her and take her home quickly before he did something he might regret. With this
in mind, he picked up speed heading for the exit.
Suddenly they hit one of the parking lot's speed
bumps.

"Eeek!" Ann said helplessly as the drinks
sloshed all over her.

Biff hit the brakes and the drinks spilled again.
"Rats!"

A plentiful supply of crushed ice lay in Ann's
lap, and her jeans and shirt were drenched with
Pepsi. "Could I have a napkin?"

Overwhelmed by remorse, Biff began pulling
paper napkins out of the fries bag and trying to
blot up some of the drink that had spilled all over
her. "I'm sorry," he muttered. "I was going too
fast. I wasn't thinking."

"It's not your fault," she protested. "The tops
weren't on tight."

He was futilely trying to blot the Pepsi off her
blouse with handfuls of napkins. He was so close
to her he could smell the clean smell of her hair.
Suddenly he turned his head and the next thing
he knew, he had forgotten all about the spilled
drink and was kissing her.

A horn complained behind them and the irri-
tated driver pulled around them with a roar,
leaving a cloud of exhaust in his wake. Biff drew
away from Ann and swallowed hard. "Maybe I'd

better go in and get some more napkins," he said. "What do you think?"

"It d-doesn't matter," she stammered. "Don't worry about it."

This is awful, Biff was thinking. I kissed her. Worse yet, I liked it. No, I loved it. I could kiss her for hours. I must be crazy. I've got to get a grip on myself.

He started up the car again and drove very slowly out of the parking lot, so slowly that when they hit the next speed bump the car only rocked gently. "I'm really sorry I spilled all the drinks," he said. "I guess I didn't realize how fast I was going."

"Really, it doesn't matter a bit." Ann-Marie was feeling slightly dazed. To think that yesterday she hadn't even been introduced to Biff and today—she had kissed him.

There was only one catch. He was still thinking she was Ann B. Somehow, she was afraid that little detail might turn out to be important.

She glanced over at him and saw that he was staring fixedly at the road ahead.

"I think movies these days are better than they used to be," she said after a moment.

"Huh? What? Oh, movies. You do?"

"There are more different kinds, you know. Sort of something for everyone. Maybe it's because of VCRs. You think?"

"I guess so," Biff said.

They sat in a rather strained silence until they reached Ann-Marie's house, and Biff pulled the car up in the driveway. He promptly hopped out and opened her car door for her, then walked beside her up to the front stoop."Well, good night," he said. He thrust his hands deep into his pockets and gazed back at the car.

"Good night," she said wistfully. He was so big to be such a gentle person, she thought. She could have stood there under the porch light all evening looking at his kind eyes and the stern eyebrows over them. She had wondered if he was going to kiss her again, but obviously, he was not. So after a moment's hesitation, she turned away from him and went in.

A minute later, she stood at the window of her darkened bedroom, pressing her nose against the windowpane and watching his car drive away.

Ann-Marie saw Felicia at church the next day. Felicia kept looking back at her, mouthing questions and peering over her hymnal with curiosity.

"What's wrong with Felicia?" asked Ann-Marie's mother.

"I think she's trying to tell me she's going to come over this afternoon," Ann-Marie replied.

While the recessional was played, the Echersleys made their customary quick exit from the church. Ann-Marie's parents only made it to church once or twice a month, and when they did come they disliked lingering after the service making what they called "social chitchat." So while others were moving back to the parish hall for coffee hour or standing in a patient line to compliment the minister on his sermon, the Echersleys had ducked out the side door and were hurrying across the lawn to their car.

"I hope you noticed the psalm today, girls," Mr. Echersley said, as he led the way at a brisk trot. "Fantastic psalm, one of the most beautiful in the language. That parallel structure that gives it its form is characteristic of Hebrew poetry. You kids should try to memorize as many psalms as you can. You want the majestic rhythms of the language to get to be second nature to you."

Ann-Marie had not particularly noticed the psalm, much less its majestic rhythms. She had other things on her mind. She was busy thinking about what she would tell Felicia when she came over that afternoon. That Felicia would come over to get a full report on her date with Biff, she had no doubt. In fact, Ann-Marie made a little bet with herself that Felicia would show up before the family got the lunch dishes cleared off the table.

Sure enough, a couple of hours later, Mrs. Echersley was just stacking the soup bowls when Felicia made her appearance.

"It's Susannah's turn for dishes," Ann-Marie pronounced, promptly dropping her napkin on the table. "Felicia and I are going to my room."

The two girls made a getaway to the bedroom, being careful to close the door behind them.

"Tell all," Felicia said dramatically, flinging herself on the bed. "Have you told him the truth yet?"

"Not exactly," Ann-Marie admitted.

Felicia sat bolt upright. "Ann-Marie!" she exclaimed. "You're going to regret this."

"I already regret it," she said. She pulled up a chair next to the bed. "You see, the thing is, Felicia, I think he really likes me. He seems drawn to me, you know? Like in *The Moth and the Flame*."

"I haven't read *The Moth and the Flame*," Felicia said in a dampening tone. "And I don't know what you mean."

"He keeps looking at me, you know? And—" she blushed "—he kissed me."

"Naturally he kissed you," said Felicia. "He thinks you're Ann B. He probably thought she expected it, a girl like her. She's probably kissed hundreds of boys. Thousands, even."

"True," Ann-Marie said, slightly chastened. "But don't you think he might be drawn to me? I'm certainly drawn to him." She stared at her sheepdog poster—I See Best with My Heart. How true. She felt she saw a deeper, more poignant meaning in those words now than she ever had before.

She looked back at Felicia with a sober expression. "I think I'm in love."

"How can you be in love? You just met the guy. *He doesn't even know who you are.*"

"I don't know why I ever tell you anything, Felicia. You are so unsympathetic."

"I am a realist. You appreciate my realism," said Felicia.

"Don't you think that people can be drawn to each other instantly? At first sight? Don't you? Honestly?"

"I suppose it's possible," conceded Felicia. "But then you don't call it love, you call it sex."

"Do you have to be so coarse?" Ann-Marie said.

"I am—"

"I know," Ann-Marie replied irritably, "a realist. You already told me."

"And don't forget he thinks you're Ann B."

"What's in a name?" Ann-Marie flung her hand out lyrically. "So he thinks my name is Ann Brierly. It's *me* he likes. It's *me* he kissed."

"Ah," said Felicia, "but it's just possible that he's drawn to you because he thinks you're Ann B., right? You know, a woman with a past may be what he craves. It's like when you're introduced to somebody and they say 'This is Ralph Birnbaum. He grows orchids.' Don't you think you react to them differently than if they tell you that Ralphie-boy is a race-car driver or a soldier of fortune or something?"

There was a silence.

"All the friends in the world I could have had," said Ann-Marie, "and I had to pick you."

"You just think I'm right, that's all," Felicia said, examining her nails complacently.

At lunch on Sunday, Biff was unusually silent.

"I think I may want to be an actress," Jenny, who was fourteen, announced. "Now listen everybody, because this is really important. I was reading the other day that all of the really famous leading ladies have unusual faces. Being pretty isn't enough. Now what I'm saying is, I think we ought to forget about these braces of mine. Not only are they absolutely gross, but look at Sigourney Weaver, look at Rosanna Arquette, look at Farrah Fawcett! They never had braces. In fact, braces could have literally—" she lowered her voice dramatically "—ruined their careers."

"No, you may not have your braces taken off, Jenny," said her mother, slicing the roast beef.

"I ran into Jerry Hodges at the club this morning," said Mr. Robertson, ignoring his daughter. "And is he ever putting on the weight. If you ask me he ought to forget the golf cart and carry those clubs. It would do him good." Mr. Robertson was reaching for the mashed potatoes but remembering the example of Jerry Hodges, he changed his mind and put down the spoon. "But that's not what I meant to say. What I wanted to tell you is he assured me the police are leaving no stone unturned. They're leaning on every known criminal in town trying to get a lead. In fact, he told me privately they're skating pretty darn close to harassment trying to shake out some information."

"Isn't that sweet of Jerry," his wife said. "I hope you told him that we appreciate it. Does he think it's somebody local, then?"

"Doesn't know. So far, no leads. But they've got to start somewhere."

"Bette Davis had those eyes, Merle Oberon had that Oriental-looking face, Grace Kelly had a lantern jaw," Jenny persisted doggedly. "I don't think you understand what I'm saying, Mom."

"I understand you perfectly, dear, and I'm very sorry to blight your career as a leading lady, but Dr. Bynum says you need braces and believe me, you are going to wear braces."

Jenny looked down and rolled her peas back and forth with her fork. Her long dark hair swung forward, obscuring Biff's view of her face, but he was pretty sure she was intently planning her next move. Jenny was never discouraged for very long.

"Have Mother and Dad got that burglar alarm put in yet?" Mr. Robertson asked his wife.

"Yes, I talked to your mother yesterday, and she said they had already accidentally set it off twice. She's afraid the neighbors may start to complain."

"At least that shows it's working," said Mr. Robertson.

"Biff are you feeling all right?" his mother asked.

"What? Oh, sure. I'm okay." Biff's mother was a tall, blond woman whose serenity was matched only by her quiet efficiency. She was the only one who really listened to what everybody in the family was saying. Biff had to admit that if asked to give a thumbnail summary of what his father and sister had said in the past week, he would have drawn a total blank. His mother, on the other hand, could have produced an up-to-date itemized list of what was on each person's mind. In addition to listening to everyone, she also kept the family calendar and reminded people of crucial appointments. Biff supposed that if she didn't keep track of everything, the whole household would fall apart. He was conscious of her eyes on him as he plowed into his mashed potatoes.

What he didn't want to explain to his mother was that he was worried about his involvement with Ron's girlfriend. He hated to admit to anybody that he'd gotten mixed up in this business and, worse yet, that he was making a mess of it. He hadn't really found out yet what was going on with Spike and Boomer, though he had at least found out that Ron's suspicions were on the right track. If he wanted to help Ron and keep Ann out of trouble, he was going to have to go further. He was going to have to figure out what Spike and Boomer were trying to get Ann mixed up in and then persuade her to stay clear, or else figure out some other way to make them leave her out of it. It gave him great satisfaction to imagine himself knocking the two boys' heads together in the course of persuading them, and he smiled a little as he took a second helping of peas.

Okay, what he should do on that score was clear enough. What was not clear was how he could do it without kissing Ann again. You only had to look at how he had slipped up and kissed her in the car to see the way that was going. So far, his self-control rated zero. And to be honest about this, she had seemed to like kissing him, too. The way she looked at him, for example— but Ron, he was forgetting the problem of Ron. Biff had to admit that Ron had had some problems in the past getting girls to take him seriously. And here was a girl he really had something going with. It would be a very low-down, mean, sneaky, dirty trick to get Ron's girl away from him while he was in Colorado. It wasn't the kind of thing you could do to your best friend. Biff ruminated on the complexities of the situation while slowly chewing his food, and his mother darted a look of concern in his direction.

At the pay phone outside Lazlo's a girl in a Mumford Athletic Department T-shirt was talking to someone while simultaneously checking her reflection in the window. She pulled a lipstick from the fringed purse that hung over her shoulder and, making a face at the window, touched up the raspberry color on her lips. Smacking her lips together once, she said into the phone, "I still don't see how they can search your house without a warrant, Boomer. It's not legal, I'm telling you. No, I don't know anything about parole. What do you think I am, a lawyer or something? Look, you worry too much." She stooped to pull up her socks, holding the phone with her chin. "Well, I don't know about that. It's not so good for me to have it because of my parents, you know. They're always poking around my things. The way my mom is she'd probably sniff it out in forty-eight hours, no kidding. She's part bloodhound. Can't you hide it at your place? I tell you, forget that. The cops aren't going to search the house."

An elderly lady wearing sensible, lace-up shoes walked past and cast an incredulous look at the absolutely identical sensible lace-up shoes worn by the girl standing at the telephone. The girl was wearing a white T-shirt, a tight skirt with a palm-leaf design and purple socks. "Teenagers," the elderly lady muttered as she passed by.

"Well, all right, all right, okay," the girl in the T-shirt was saying. "Quit worrying about it. I'll think of something."

Chapter Five

Monday afternoon, Ann-Marie settled down on her bed with *Sonnets from the Portuguese* and a salami sandwich. She liked the way the title on the book's cover was circled by a wreath of pink and lavender flowers. Even better, she liked the topic—love. She wished to explore the topic of love exhaustively, to examine it from every angle. *The Moth and the Flame*, for example, gave one angle. *Sonnets from the Portuguese* gave yet another. Ann-Marie's instinctive response when something interested her was to read up on it. In this way she had picked up so much miscellaneous information that she was a very formidable opponent at Trivial Pursuit.

She was convinced that paperbacks multiplied secretly in her closet like rabbits because they seemed to spill out everywhere. And always two stacks of hardcovers stood on the floor by her dresser, a tall stack of books to go back to the library and a smaller stack of books yet to be read. More than once she had wished that the library provided wheelbarrows for its patrons.

One of the things in her otherwise boring life that she was secretly proud of happened in the sixth grade, the day that Allen Fincher had run from room to room flashing a T-shirt with an obscene message at each classroom door. Ann-Marie had been, she believed, the only kid in her class who read fast enough to catch the message. She naturally did not tell anybody what the T-shirt said. That would have been embarrassing. But privately she was very proud of her speed-reading.

"'How do I love thee? Let me count the ways,'" she read. She laid the book down and took a bite of salami. Biff, Biff, Biff, she thought. *Je t'adore.* When she finished college, she might very well live in Paris and speak French always. Unless, that is, she decided to live in Berlin, where, though they were short on romance, she understood they did have first-class salami.

Felicia is right, she thought. I am probably attracted to her realism. That's because of the two, utterly different sides of my personality, the realistic—symbolized by this sandwich—and the romantic—symbolized by the book now lying facedown on my tummy. The romantic side of me murmurs Biff, Biff, Biff unceasingly like a passionate, searching spirit. The realistic side tells me I've gotten myself in one heck of a pickle.

It would have been nice to know what on earth Ann B. was up to with Spike and Boomer. She knew Ann B. just well enough to know it could be almost anything, which made her fairly uneasy.

The phone on the bedside table began to ring, but Ann-Marie was so engrossed in her thoughts she barely heard it. It was only on the fourth ring that she suddenly realized it could be Biff and snatched at it.

"Hello?"

"Ann? This is Biff."

"Oh, Biff," she said, melting backward onto the bed. "Hi!"

"You aren't busy or anything right now, are you?"

"Oh, no. I was just sitting here reading. How are you?"

"Okay. Listen, we need to talk. I'd like to take you out to dinner, okay?"

"That sounds great."

"Is tonight okay? We'll go over to Bienvenue."

Ann-Marie had never been to Bienvenue Country Club because her parents were opposed to country clubs on principle, but she couldn't wait to taste its amenities. She could check with Felicia about what to wear. Felicia's parents did not have nearly so many inconvenient principles as Ann-Marie's.

"I'll pick you up in a few hours," Biff was saying. "Say seven?"

A few hours? Only a few hours until the date of her lifetime? She had imagined a preparation for it a little more along the time scheme outlined in Marvell's "To His Coy Mistress": an hour to enamel each fingernail, a week to perfect the mascara, an aeon to worry about what she was going to say. And the more she thought about it, she didn't quite like the sound of this dinner. What did they suddenly need to *talk* about? Wasn't it enough to sit in the candlelight looking into each other's eyes? That would certainly have been enough for her. She didn't need to talk. She had the uncomfortable feeling that talking could only lead to Spike and Boomer. "Okay," she said hesitantly.

When Biff swung by the house at seven, Ann-Marie showed no sign of the uneasiness churning inside her other than the anxious looks she kept sending his way.

She was wearing a delicate, off-the-shoulder white dress with sheer bone stockings, and she had parted her hair on the side and pulled it back on the other side with a pretty comb. Dressed this way, Ann-Marie felt prepared for the music and dancing that, Felicia had assured her during a frantic phone call, was a nightly feature of the Azure Room at Bienvenue. She was prepared for dancing, all right. What she was not prepared for was the talking part.

She knew that she should tell Biff she was not Ann B., but she couldn't bring herself to do it. How could she tell him that she was not only an ingenue but a liar as well?

And what if Felicia was right and Biff was only attracted to her because he thought she was Ann B.? She didn't think she could stand to have Biff vanish suddenly from her life, to know she would never see that uncertain little smile of his again or feel his big, warm hand enveloping hers.

She was in a mess, all right. Never, never would she have thought she would have anything in common with Ann B. And now, not only was she being as dishonest as Ann B., she was actually *being* Ann B. The clichés she had run across in pulp fiction, such as "stolen kisses" and "living a lie" didn't sound funny to her anymore. She knew precisely what they meant.

"I got a postcard from Ron today," Biff said.

Ann-Marie's head jerked in alarm. She had understood that this Ron person was out in the wilderness somewhere and totally, but totally, out of the picture. She had been counting on it. "H-how did he manage that?" she asked. "I thought that with this Outward Bound program they drop you out in the middle of a thousand-acre forest."

"I think he mailed it from the Denver airport before he hooked up with them," said Biff. "He asked me how you were getting along."

Ann-Marie thought this Ron sounded like a dope—going out with Ann B., doing dangerous things just for the fun of it. "I don't understand why people want to do that kind of thing," Ann-Marie muttered.

"Oh, well, you know Ron," said Biff. "Always trying to prove something."

But I don't, thought Ann-Marie, that's the trouble. I don't know Ron. It was definitely time to change the subject.

Biff was sitting in embarrassed silence, reminding himself than Ann was Ron's girl and that he shouldn't have made that crack about Ron.

Ann-Marie gripped her purse tightly and tried to think serene, blue and green thoughts the way her mother was always advising her to do. This Ron person was out in Colorado and with any luck wouldn't be back for weeks. She would just enjoy the moment and worry about Ron later. "This will be fun," she said. "I've never been to Bienvenue Country Club."

Biff looked at her in surprise. "But I thought you'd been with Ron lots of times."

"In the summer," she said hastily. "That's what I was going to say." She was going to have to remember to quit volunteering things. It was far too risky. Already she could see that Biff was giving her a funny look.

They turned up the winding drive marked with the sign Bienvenue Country Club, Members Only, and Ann-Marie reminded herself that she would have to be sure not to ask where the ladies' room was, since she had been here so very many times before with Ron.

Biff found a parking place near the entrance and got out to open the car door for her. They mounted the steps at the entrance and then, going in, moved past some potted palms into the club's lobby. Ann-Marie could hear strings and a clarinet playing in a room to her right. Members of a wedding party were milling about in the lobby, the bride recognizable by her cream-colored suit and the flowers in her hair. Several children were huddled at the edge of the wedding party, two girls of ten or twelve looking uncomfortable in taffeta dresses and a boy somewhat younger, dressed in an obviously new suit. Judging from their dreadful expressions, AnnMarie was certain these kids had just unwillingly become stepbrothers and -sisters.

The hostess, a young woman carrying a clipboard and tottering on precariously high heels, began leading the wedding party into the Azure Room. Having deposited them there, she promptly came back for Biff and Ann-Marie. "Two?" she said, smiling brightly.

They followed her into the room past a small forest of potted palms. Ann-Marie could see that on the other side of the room the musicians stood before a series of glass doors that looked out on the terrace and the golf course beyond, where a pennant fluttered in the breeze. She could see a foursome standing on a putting green.

Artificial twilight reigned inside the restaurant. Above a collection of small round tables, which were draped in white linen, the chandeliers shone brightly, their tiny points of light and their crystal pendants reflected over and over

again in the ornate gilt mirrors that lined the blue
walls.

Ann-Marie noticed that the wedding party was
seated at several tables in small groups, and considering the looks on the faces of the stepchildren, she concluded that this was probably a
good plan. Separating the stepchildren from each
other by a six-foot fence would have been an even
better move.

Biff pulled out her chair for her, and she saw
that there was a vase of blue cornflowers and a
wisp of fern on their table. As she sat down, she
touched one of the flowers delicately with her
fingertips to assure herself that it was real. It was.
She began to cheer up. So what if she was an impostor? She might as well enjoy herself, right?

"The food here is not that great," Biff said,
opening a menu. "But you can usually count on
the steak."

Sounds of strained hilarity were coming from
the wedding party nearby.

A waitress wearing a white apron appeared to
take their order. "I think I'll have the *coquilles
St. Jacques*," Ann-Marie said.

"It's probably frozen," Biff warned her. "You
know, like a TV dinner."

Ann-Marie would have liked to explain to him
that a lifetime spent living on health food had left
her a sucker for anything, absolutely anything

smothered in cream sauce and artificial preservatives, but she remembered that she had decided to try not to volunteer information. "I like seafood," she said, folding her menu and putting it down.

Biff ordered steak with all the trimmings, and the waitress left. A waiter appeared at Ann's side with a bottle, wrapped in a cloth napkin, which he began pouring into her glass. She watched with fascination when she saw that little bubbles were clinging to the sides of her glass.

"We're not with the wedding party," Biff told the waiter sharply. He picked up Ann-Marie's glass and gave it back to the waiter.

"Excuse me, sir," said the waiter, taking the glass from him and moving away.

Ann-Marie watched sadly as her very first chance to taste champagne was carried away on a tray. It appeared that Biff was one of those people like her parents with inconvenient principles. She glanced over at Biff and saw that he was sagging in his seat with the sort of look that might have been worn by the people who had had reservations on the *Titanic* but had taken a later boat instead.

She took a sip of iced water and looked at him over the rim of her glass.

"Are you a Methodist?" she hazarded.

He shook his head.

"Baptist, then?"

"I just don't think underage people should drink," he said. "It's against the law."

"Not even champagne?" asked Ann-Marie.

"Not even champagne," he assured her.

Champagne had featured largely in *The Moth and the Flame* and Ann-Marie would have loved to have had just one little sip of it, just to see what it was like, but she admired Biff for having principles. It confirmed her belief that he was a person of the highest moral standards. Unfortunately she hated to think what a person of the highest moral standards would think of the deception she was now engaged in.

Laughter pealed from behind her, and Ann-Marie glanced back to see the bride sharing a joke with two boutonnieres and a couple of lace-trimmed dresses. At a table slightly to the left of them, the stepchildren glared at each other.

The quartet began playing a fox-trot and the bride and groom and several members of the wedding party got up to dance. "Do you like to dance?" Ann-Marie asked, looking at Biff hopefully.

He didn't answer but got up and silently pulled out her chair. Ann-Marie wished she knew what she had done to make him look at her like that. She hadn't actually drunk any of the champagne, after all. Silently he took her hand and they began dancing. Then Biff looked down at her and gave her one of his lopsided little smiles. Suddenly Ann-Marie began to feel as if her feet were moving of their own volition, and she had to firmly stifle an impulse to murmur some of Elizabeth Barrett Browning's better lines in Biff's ear.

How do I love thee, she thought, looking into Biff's brown eyes. Let me count the ways! I love your beautiful eyes. I love the way the short-cropped hair is brushed back at your temples and I love your broad shoulders and the faint pink look of your ears and the freckles on your nose. I love every dark rumpled hair on your wonderful head. I even love your ridiculous high principles.

"Nice music," she said. She suddenly looked down at her feet, embarrassed by her thoughts.

Biff touched her cheek with one finger, and when she looked up he smiled at her.

"You are just so different from the way I expected," he said. "I didn't think—well, never mind about that."

"You didn't think what?"

"I didn't think I would like you this much," said Biff, flushing a little.

"I like you, too," said Ann-Marie.

"Look, Ann, whatever it is you're mixed up in with Spike and Boomer, you've got to get out of

it. You haven't done something really, well, serious, have you?''

Ann-Marie blinked rapidly as panic swept over
her. How had they gone from ''I like you,'' to
Spike and Boomer in one step?

''I d-don't know,'' she stuttered. ''I mean, I
don't know what you're talking about.''

He held her tight against him. ''Look, if you
want to straighten out your life, it's never too
late,'' he said gruffly. ''Maybe I can help. Just
tell me what's going on.''

''Nothing's going on!''

Biff looked at her sadly.

''I think that's our food,'' said Ann-Marie,
relieved to see the waitress approach their table
with a steaming tray.

When they sat down, Ann-Marie took a deep
breath. ''Look, Biff, there's something I should
tell you,'' she said.

Biff was engaged in lifting a metal cover off
the broccoli au gratin, but he paused, holding it
in the air, and looked at her.

The boy in the new suit chose this moment to
heave his cake at one of his new stepsisters. There
was a clatter of crockery and silverware as the
more alert of the adults leaped up to restore order. ''Mo-ther,'' wailed the victim, wiping icing
off her ear.

"Will you look at that?" Biff said, aghast. "Nobody teaches kids table manners anymore."

The combatants were dragged off to bathrooms by their respective parents, and the noise from the wedding party became muted.

Biff forcibly wrenched his attention from the drama at the nearby tables and fixed Ann-Marie with his eyes. "Don't pay any attention to them," he said. "Go on with what you were telling me."

"Nothing," said Ann-Marie, looking at him with frightened eyes. "I wasn't saying anything. It's only that I don't know anything about Spike and Boomer, Biff. And it's not the way you think. Believe me."

He reached for her hand.

"Do you think that something can be just meant to be?" he asked in a low voice, a troubled look on his face. "You know, like sometimes two people just have something, it's hard to explain, a feeling that you know somebody, not déjà vu exactly."

"As if you've known each other in some other life?" Ann-Marie suggested.

"I don't believe in that junk," he said, "but what I'm talking about is a feeling that you really are close to a person. It's like the two of you have got something that's so important that everything else just fades out."

"Sure," she said, smiling at him shyly.

He dropped her hand and began cutting at his steak. "A hypothetical situation, of course," he said.

She ate a spoonful of the creamed scallops. "I've read about things like that," she said. "I expect it would be a good thing to research, don't you know? These, uh, feelings that people get, I mean. Probably not much is really known about that kind of thing."

"It's crazy," said Biff, regarding his steak with a fierce look.

"But I thought you just said—"

"What people ought to do is to get a grip on themselves and forget all that stuff," said Biff.

"I don't agree," said Ann-Marie. The *co-quilles St. Jacques weren't bad*. Biff had been right about them being sort of like a TV dinner, but she liked TV dinners. The tastiness of the *coquilles St. Jacques* reinforced her faith in her own judgment. "I don't agree at all," she repeated more firmly. "If all people did was to forget their feelings and get a grip on themselves, we wouldn't have any art, or music, or much science." She hesitated. "Or any love, either." She hurried on, "What about Leonardo? What about Marie Curie? People have to have feelings and ambitions and dreams and ideas—all those things—before they can begin to do anything that's really important or difficult. They have to want to do it and think of doing it first, you see."

Biff was looking bewildered. "You lost me," he said.

"I read a lot," Ann-Marie said, blushing.

"That's funny. I got the idea from Ron that you hated school and all that," he said.

"Well," she said quickly, "school is awfully rigid, you know. Not much outlet for creativity. It's okay, really, but I like to go beyond the kind of thing they do in school. I guess that's what Ron was talking about."

"You know, I'm beginning to think Ron doesn't really know you at all."

Ann-Marie blanched. "What makes you say that?"

"I think he's got the wrong idea about you. Maybe you two just aren't on the same wavelength. Ron's a great guy, but he doesn't seem to realize that girls can think, if you know what I mean. I think it sort of warps the way he sees things, sometimes."

Ann-Marie studied her plate.

"Not that I mean to be bad-mouthing Ron," Biff said, suddenly ashamed. "Heck, he's my best friend. And, of course, he's your—well, anyway, old Ron is a great guy. The best."

"Oh, yes," Ann-Marie said weakly.

Biff slathered sour cream and butter on his baked potato and proceeded to attack it. A moment later he turned his attention back to the huge steak.

"That steak really looks good," said Ann-Marie, impressed by his appetite. Life with her father the vegetarian had done nothing to prepare her for Biff's rampant carnivorousness. His steak looked to her like the sort of thing that one person could never eat in one sitting. She could only imagine that it would be turned into progressively smaller doggy bags, day after day, until at the end of a week of working on it, the person who had rashly ordered it would finish off the last bite never wanting to see a steak again.

"Want some?" he asked. "There's plenty." He cut off a piece and put it on her plate. As his arm brushed her hand, he froze a minute, then looked down at his food and chewed with a vengeance.

"I do a lot of weight lifting and jogging," he explained, a second later. "When school starts I'll be back in football again, and I don't like to let myself get too out of shape over the summer. It's just too tough to whip yourself back into shape if you've let yourself get slack."

It was one of fate's comic little tricks, Ann-Marie thought, that she should be so utterly besotted with someone who was, to put it bluntly, a jock. She had a strong intuition that Biff would never be very interested in Elizabeth Barrett Browning's poems, and she didn't even care. She leaned her chin on her hand and looked into his eyes while he outlined his plans for keeping in shape over the summer, which ranged from working in his uncle's construction firm to a system of hoisting weights that Ann-Marie never really got straight. She was not interested in his weights, but she listened patiently because she intuitively understood that he was talking about the fine points of training solely to keep from talking about him and her. She could respect that. Normally she didn't believe in rushing things. The only thing that really bothered her was that unless they rushed things, she would never get to any of the good stuff, such as how he worshiped the ground she walked on, until he had found out who she really was and had said he never wanted to see her again. She stifled a sad little sigh.

When they left the club, it was dark outside and since the lot was lit only by the light cast from the club's entrance, Biff took her arm and guided her along the stepping-stones to the car. When he got in the car, she looked toward him hopefully, but he ignored her and concentrated on backing out of the parking space. Since he had amazed her by finishing off every morsel of the huge steak, she decided that very likely the reason he was suddenly so silent was he was suffering from acute indigestion.

A little later, they were standing again under the porch light at 933 Wickerberry Road. "It was a lovely dinner," said Ann-Marie.

"Next time try the steak," said Biff.

Ann-Marie dimpled. "Well, good night," she said. She turned toward the door.

"Ann?" he said.

She wheeled around.

"What do you think about this stuff about how we sort of like each other."

Her smile was like a sunburst. "I think it's great," she said.

Biff's last conscious thought before he took her in his arms and kissed her was that Ron would just have to lump it.

Chapter Six

Biff was sitting in the kitchen having a little after-dinner snack of a ham sandwich and milk. He was feeling considerably more cheerful than he had felt in days. He thought he had it all figured out at last. Somehow or another Ann must have gotten wind of something Spike and Boomer were up to and they had sworn her to secrecy. Now that he thought of it, that would explain everything. It would explain why Ron had the feeling something was going on between the three of them and it would explain why Ann wouldn't tell Biff about it. It wasn't that she didn't trust him, but that she had given her word. Realizing that made him feel a lot better. He had felt from the start that though Ann might have shown a little bad judgment in the past, she could not possibly be mixed up in anything really shady. You only had to look at the girl to know she was the soul of honor, her eyes were so clear and innocent, her mouth so sweet and sensitive. It was the sort of mouth you just wanted to touch, to trace with your fingertips, to kiss.

"Ethel Rountree tells me she saw you at the club the other night with a girl," Biff's mother said, drying a pot. "I thought you and Cynthia had broken up."

Biff took his feet down from the kitchen chair and assumed a more alert posture. This could get sticky.

"Cynthia? Mom, Cynthia is history."

"She seemed like such a nice girl to me," said his mother.

"You've got to be kidding. She cracks her knuckles!"

"Oh, dear. That could be serious. Well, who was this girl at the club, then? You must really like her to take her to the Azure Room."

"Just a friend," Biff said casually. He figured that so far he was handling this whole thing pretty well. "Friend" hit just the right note, he thought.

"Well, do I know her? Do I know her mother? What's her name?"

"You don't know her," Biff said, standing up. "I think I'll go scrub out those garbage cans now before it gets dark." Since his mother had been bugging him for a week to scrub out the garbage cans, he was sure he had picked the ideal exit line. When he ambled out the back door he was whistling a tune.

Biff's father came into the kitchen and threw the newspaper on the kitchen table. "Did you read Armbruster's editorial?" he asked. "I may just write to him. Not that anybody could get through to that numbskull. He's a congenital idiot, that's his trouble."

Biff's mother for once hadn't heard her husband. She was looking out the kitchen window, watching Biff dragging a garbage can over within reach of the hoses. "Phil, I'm worried about Biff."

Jenny pushed open the kitchen door. "I need a ride over to Northgreen," she said. "Susannah and I are supposed to practice our duet."

"Your mother and I are talking," said Mr. Robertson. "Go ask Biff to drive you."

After Jenny left, Mr. Robertson leaned toward his wife. "What do you mean 'worried'?" he asked in a low voice. "You don't mean... drugs?"

"No, no," she said. "Not that. I think it's a girl, Phil. He's seeing somebody he won't tell me about. I don't like it."

"He's just growing up, that's all."

"He's never done this before. You know how those girls he dates are always in and out of the house when they're on their way to ball games and so forth. It seems to me the poor things always end up carrying Biff's gym bag. But this one he takes to the Azure Room."

"I hope he didn't sign my name to the check," said her husband, picking up the newspaper.

"I tell you, Phil, there's something wrong. He's not himself. Something's on his mind."

"Love, probably," he replied. "I was always in love at his age. Did I ever tell you about Maggie Owen?"

"Frequently. Don't you even care that your son may be getting involved with some girl who is completely unsuitable, someone he is even afraid to mention to us?"

"You may have it wrong there, honey," said her husband, grinning. "Maybe it's us he's ashamed of and not her."

"You aren't listening to me, Phil. I'm telling you, I think something is wrong."

"Okay. I'll ask around. Somebody must know this girl."

The kitchen door swung open. "Biff say's he's scrubbing garbage cans and to go away and leave him alone," said Jenny.

Mr. Robertson got up. "Okay, hotshot. Calm down. I'll take you."

When Susannah and Jenny were practicing their flute duet in the Echersleys' living room that evening, Ann-Marie glanced in the room and had the brief sensation that there was something familiar about the girl in the braces with the long dark hair, but the feeling of recognition was gone in an instant. She decided her nerves were shot. She was imagining things. The tension of pretending to be Ann B., never knowing when Biff would find out about it, was driving her over the edge. Her greatest fear was that one day Biff would walk into Lazlo's and would spot the real Ann B. sitting at the bar in one of her Mumford Athletic Department T-shirts. Then he would instantly see he had the wrong girl, and she wouldn't even have a chance to explain anything.

Was there any way out of her dilemma? Suppose she wrote a series of anonymous letters, each one leading a little closer to the truth. Would that sort of prepare Biff? Or maybe she could put to him a hypothetical situation about a girl pretending to be another girl and just see how he reacted. Maybe he wouldn't think it was so awful after all, and then she would tell him everything and her troubles would be over.

"Ann-Marie!" her mother called. "Come here for a minute."

She found her mother in the kitchen soaking a papier-mâché mixture in a large bowl. "Martha Brierly called me a little while ago," said her mother, vigorously kneading the mixture. "You know Charles is at home now, but he still needs round-the-clock nursing. Martha can't get out of the house at all unless someone comes and sits with him."

Ann-Marie began hoping she wasn't going to be asked to go sit with Mr. Brierly. She was not the sort of person who was at home in a sickroom. Actually she tended to feel sick to her stomach at the sight of tubes and oxygen tents.

"So you can imagine," Mrs. Echersley went on, "Martha was relieved when some friends of theirs offered to take Ann to Disney World with them. They have a daughter about Ann's age, so going would be fun for Ann and, more important, that would be one less thing for Martha to worry about. Ann's supposed to leave tomorrow on the train, and I was wondering if you could drive her to the station."

"I'll say! I mean, of course, Mom. I'd be glad to help out."

"I'd do it myself," said Mrs. Echersley, dumping the papier-mâché mixture onto a sheet of waxed paper. "But I have a meeting of the City Hall Preservation Society at two. You can use my car, and I'll have Toni Hamill give me a lift to the meeting."

"Don't worry about it, Mom. I'd be *happy* to do it."

Her mother grinned up at her. "Glad to get rid of her, huh?"

"In more ways than you know," Ann-Marie muttered.

"There's just one thing, sweetheart," her mother said. "Don't let her out of your sight. I want you to wait at the station with her and actually watch her get on that train. Just to be on the safe side, you'd better watch the train until it picks up speed."

"Do you think she's going to try something?" asked Ann-Marie.

"No, I don't have any reason to think that. Martha says Ann really wants to go to Disney World. It's just that when I tell Martha we put her on the train, I want to be sure she really *got* on the train and not have her turn up in Kuala Lumpur next week. Do you understand?"

"I follow you."

"At the train's next stop these friends of the Brierlys will meet up with her, and after that she's their responsibility."

"Thank goodness," said Ann-Marie.

The phone rang and Ann-Marie's mother reached for it. "Hello? Just a minute and I'll get her." She covered the receiver with her hand. "It's Biff again," she said.

"I'll take it in my room," Ann-Marie said, hurrying out.

Once in her room she threw herself on her bed and reached for the phone, not bothering to turn on the lights. She liked best to just lie there in the dark and listen to Biff's voice. "Biff?" she said.

"Hey," he said. "What are you up to?"

"Nothing much. How about you?"

"Spent the whole day sweeping floors. I'm getting pretty fed up with it. I thought I'd be outside all the time, hammering, pouring cement, things like that."

"Working for family is always like that," said Ann-Marie. "You wouldn't believe the time I spent last summer pricing and bagging sunflower seeds."

"What is it your dad does?"

Too late Ann-Marie remembered that she had decided not to volunteer any information. All Biff had to do was to ask just about anybody and he would learn that Ann B.'s father owned a hardware store. She did not think they carried sunflower seeds in hardware stores.

"He's in business for himself," said Ann-Marie in a muted voice. She hated lying to Biff and couldn't bring herself to say outright that her father owned a hardware store and sold sunflower seeds on the side.

She was glad when Biff started talking about his awful third-grade teacher who made the boys take turns staying in and sweeping the floor during recess. Fortunately, awful teachers was a vast, even a bottomless subject and they happily compared their most horrible experiences for some time.

After they hung up, Ann-Marie lay on the bed in the dark, thinking of how she loved to hear Biff's voice. She had a perfect relationship with him, she told herself, except that it only had a shelf life of, give or take, three weeks. She wasn't sure exactly how long because she didn't know when Ron was getting back in town and she couldn't very well ask Biff.

But at least she could have these few precious moments of stolen bliss—marred only by her being practically a nervous wreck. And after all, she should look on the bright side. She was getting Ann B. out of the way for a while. That should help. At least she could quit worrying about Biff running into Ann B. at Lazlo's.

The next day at quarter after one, Ann-Marie took the car next door to pick up Ann B. She was relieved to see that the girl was not wearing one of the infamous Mumford Athletic Department T-shirts. She was dressed in a black sarong skirt, elevator shoes and a Mickey Mouse T-shirt. Ann-Marie hopped out of the car and unlocked the hatchback for her. "Need help with those suitcases?" she asked, glancing at the three cases—an attaché case, a suitcase and a canvas carryall.

"Nah. You go on and get in," said Ann B., hoisting the larger of the cases into the hatchback.

Ann-Marie got back into the car. She noticed there was no longer any mention of Ann B.'s bad back. In the rearview mirror she could see the top of Ann B.'s head and the twisted pink scarf that served to hold her unruly hair in place as she bent over to arrange the luggage in back.

After a while, Ann-Marie called back, "Are you sure you don't need any help?"

Ann B. looked up, startled. "Nope," she said. "All set." She slammed the hatchback closed and came around to get in the passenger's seat.

"So," said Ann-Marie, "you're going to Disney World."

"Yup," Ann B. replied.

That was the sum total of their conversation until Ann-Marie drove up in the parking lot at the train station.

Getting out to unlock the hatchback, Ann-Marie remembered how poky Ann B. had been about stashing the luggage in the back. So as soon as she had the hatchback opened, she grabbed the largest of the cases to carry herself and began moving at once toward the entrance to the station, casting a glance over her shoulder to make sure Ann B. was following her. The last thing she wanted was for Ann B. to miss the train.

The small train station dated from the glory days of railroading. It had comfortable long polished wood benches in the center of the room, and the walls were lined with posters depicting some of Amtrak's more glamorous destinations—pictures of Palm Beach and New Orleans bathed in sunshine. But the floors of the place were grimy and the doors to the rest rooms looked like large green lockers that had been kicked again and again.

Ann B. plopped down on a bench and began picking at her front teeth with a fingernail. "You don't have to wait," said Ann B. "You go on."

"Oh, I insist," said Ann-Marie. She sat down and folded her arms as if fully prepared to wait a decade.

After a moment, Ann B. got up to walk toward the water fountain at the other end of the room. She bent over to drink for a moment, then moved to the pay phone near the ticket window and fished some change out of her pocketbook. Observing her from the distance, Ann-Marie decided that she would have been suspicious of this girl even without knowing that she had every reason to be. Something about the total lack of anxiety on Ann B.'s face and the little smile that tended to play over her lips, suggested to Ann-Marie that this was not a person you could trust. Who could she be calling? Not her mother, that was for sure. Maybe her bookie, thought Ann-Marie.

At the other end of the room, Ann B. turned her back to Ann Marie and began speaking into the receiver. "It's okay," she was saying. "I fixed it. I left it in her car. Piece of cake. She lives in that white house next door to me and the car's an old, beat-up Mazda, you can't miss it. All you've got to do is go get it as soon as the coast is clear. I stuck it under the lining of the hatchback. Look, it's okay, Boomer. You gotta do something about all that worrying. It's dumb to worry all the time. It's bad for you."

A whistle blew as the Silver Meteor announced its arrival. Ann B. quickly glanced back over her shoulder and saw that Ann-Marie had lifted the suitcase and was heading toward her.

"Gotta go," said Ann B. into the receiver. "Keep your shirt on. Maybe I'll bring you some mouse ears, huh? Bye."

She picked up the attaché case and the canvas carryall and walked with Ann-Marie out onto the windy train platform. Once there, Ann-Marie shrank from the huge locomotive as with ear-shattering metallic shrieks it pulled itself to a halt in front of them. But Ann B. looked up at the train undisturbed. She regarded it, as she regarded most things, with general indifference. A small smile played over her lips.

When the train had stopped, Ann-Marie handed the heavy suitcase up to the conductor, who leaned over and held his hand down to help Ann B. up the steps.

When she reached the top, Ann B. looked down at Ann-Marie with that characteristic slight smile of hers, then stepped back and disappeared into the darkness behind her.

Seeing the last of Ann B., Ann-Marie suddenly felt lighthearted. She stepped back on the platform so she could get a view of the length of the train to make sure Ann B. wasn't getting off at the other end of the car. She couldn't see the other side of the train, of course, but since a freight train was rocketing past on the second track at the moment, she was fairly sure Ann B. wasn't escaping by that route. Ann-Marie breathed a sigh of satisfaction. She would be able to tell her mother in good conscience that she had watched Ann B. truly steam out of the station.

The Silver Meteor, which only paused briefly at Farmingdale, immediately began gathering speed again, and soon its gleaming length was roaring out of the station. Watching the train go past and then a few minutes later slowly grow smaller in the distance, Ann-Marie felt like leaping up and clicking her heels with joy. She's gone, she thought. She's out of here! With a brief feeling of pity for unsuspecting Disney World, she turned and headed back to her car.

Chapter Seven

Ann-Marie was not sure exactly when she began to have the feeling she was being watched, but not long after seeing Ann B. off to Disney World, she realized she had gotten in the habit of checking behind her to see if she was being followed.

Monday, when she was helping her mother unload the groceries, she spotted a van parked down the street.

"Do you see that van?" she asked, staring at it.

"Watch out for the eggs, sweetheart," her mother said, embracing a grocery bag. By balancing a mesh bag of potatoes on one knee Mrs. Echersley finally succeeded in hooking the bag's string over her hand. "What van?" she grunted, as she staggered in the direction of the front door.

"I think it was there yesterday, too," said Ann-Marie. "The Hotchkisses don't have a van, do they?"

"They probably have relatives visiting," her mother replied. "Would you get the door?"

Ann-Marie, poising a bag of groceries on one hip, opened the door. "Seems funny to me that they don't pull into the driveway," she muttered.

"That reminds me, pull the car up into the garage for me," Mrs. Echersley said. "And be sure to lock up. I don't want any of the neighborhood kids getting at that blowtorch."

Ann-Marie put her bag of groceries down by the door. When she went out to move the car, her eyes were drawn again toward the van. Its rear windows had a screaming eagle design painted over them but even though she couldn't see inside the van, Ann-Marie had the uneasy feeling that someone was in there looking at her.

Slamming the hatchback of the Mazda shut, she drove the car into the garage. Then she closed the garage door and locked it. She didn't understand this feeling she had that she was being followed.

Late that afternoon, Biff accepted a collect call from Colorado. "Ron, old buddy," he said heartily, "how's it going? Broken any bones yet?"

"It's great, man. I love it. This is a real breakthrough for me, you know? I'm pushing my horizons out in all directions. Watch out, ain't nothing I can't do, right? So how's it going with Ann, huh? I've been getting this funny feeling, and it's so strong I can't sleep nights for thinking about it. You wouldn't believe what I went through to get to this phone. Fording creeks, fighting off bears, the works. So what's the word?"

"Nothing much," said Biff.

"You're keeping something from me, aren't you? Give it to me straight, Biff. I can take it. What's wrong?"

"Nothing's wrong. I think you got the wrong end of the stick about that stuff with Spike and Boomer, no kidding. I mean, think about it, man. What would a girl like Ann be doing mixed up with that pair?"

There was a moment's silence. Then Ron said, "You sound funny, Biff. You know how I can always tell when something's on your mind. What's the matter? Go on and give it to me. I've rappelled down a dam, I'm drownproofed, I've climbed peaks. I'm tough. You think I'm going to crumble if you give it to me straight? You got me all wrong."

Right, thought Biff. I've got to be double-crossing the only guy in the country who can do mental telepathy over AT&T lines. He sighed. Okay, so maybe it was better to tell him now.

"Look, I know you aren't going to like this, Ron, and I feel pretty rotten about it myself, but Ann and I have sort of got something going."

"What?" Ron shrieked.

Biff held the receiver away from his ear and winced. When he returned it to his ear, a stream of invective was still pouring out of the phone. "Some friend you turned out to be," Ron said bitterly when he finally managed to spit out a coherent sentence. "To think that I trusted you. Boy, was I dumb. You just had to cut me out, didn't you, Biff? It's not enough that you've got all these girls throwing their bodies down under your feet night and day, you've got to go after my girl. You know something? That's sick. That's really sick. What's your problem, man? And don't think I'm just going to sit here and take it, either. I'll have something to say to you when I get home. And don't go thinking I believe you, either. Because I don't believe a word of it."

The phone clicked. "Ron?" Biff said weakly. But Ron had hung up.

That night when he picked up Ann, he was unusually subdued.

"Is something wrong, Biff?"

"No, nothing's wrong." Why does everybody keep asking me if anything's wrong? Nothing's wrong. Nothing."

Nothing except he'd double-crossed his best friend and he was going out with a girl he couldn't even tell his parents about. Biff realized that it was no accident he was taking Ann to places like the Azure Room and Sam's sandwich shop over on the north side. Any place was fine as long as it was a place he wasn't likely to run into anybody he knew. He remembered that when he found out Ron was going out with the notorious Ann Brierly he had figured Ron was the worst kind of sucker. He didn't like the idea that his friends would be thinking the same thing about him.

"Ron called up this afternoon," he growled. "I told him about us."

Ann looked at him timidly.

"Doesn't it even bother you to throw poor old Ron over like that? He was really upset, I can tell you. It was pitiful."

"Well, it's not as if Ron and I were married," Ann-Marie said with spirit. At least, she thought, I don't suppose Ron and Ann B. are married. With Ann B. you never could be sure.

"Yeah, I guess you're right," said Biff. He added gloomily, "He'll probably try to punch me out when he gets back."

Ann clutched at his arm. "You don't think he'll hurt you, do you?"

"Nah, not likely."

Later that night when Ann and Biff pulled up into the Echersleys' driveway, Biff's headlights suddenly transfixed a figure standing at the garage door. The guy's arms flew out in a gesture of surprise, and Biff saw the headlights glimmer on something that could have been a screwdriver. But in the blink of an eye, the figure had turned and darted out of range of the headlights.

"Who was that?" Biff asked sharply.

"I don't know," Ann whispered.

Biff jumped out of the car, and Ann-Marie could hear his steps crunching on the gravel of the drive as he charged after the guy into the darkness. She leaned over and locked the car doors, then sat shivering, wishing Biff had not gone after whoever it was.

A moment later, Biff came back. "Lost him," he said, opening her door. "Looked to me like the guy was trying to break into your garage. That's sure stealing a car the hard way. I wonder why he'd want to do that with all the cars parked out on the street, some of them with their keys in them, even.''

"Maybe he was after Mom's tools. She keeps all her art equipment out there. That's why we always keep the garage locked."

"Maybe," said Biff, frowning. Then he caught a glimpse of Ann's frightened face. "Hey, don't worry about it," he said, reaching for her. He pulled her up out of the car and held her close to him. "These sneak thieves are all over the place. Mostly they're pretty harmless." He kissed her ear. "Okay?"

She smiled weakly. "Okay," she said. "I guess you're right. But you know something, Biff? Lately I've had the feeling somebody's watching me."

"Huh?"

"You know, watching me, following me. I keep looking behind me. It's as if I sort of hear somebody, but I never quite catch him. And for a couple of days there was this van parked a little ways down the street."

"Hey, you're letting your imagination run away with you."

"I guess so," she said doubtfully.

The idea that someone was watching her might have been nothing but her imagination, but when her parents drove across state at the end of the week to take Susannah to music camp, Ann-Marie did not for a minute consider spending that night alone in the house. "I'll stay over at Felicia's," she told her mother.

"That's a good idea," her mother said, folding a nightshirt to add to her overnight case.

"Maybe Felicia and I will drive over to the lake Saturday.

"Fine," said her mother. "You can drive the Mazda. It's got plenty of gas in it. I know you're really bowled over by Biff, sweetheart, but it's good not to lose touch with your friends. Believe me, boys come and go, but your friends stay friends forever."

Ann-Marie didn't have to be reminded about how boys come and go. She expected Biff to be going any day now, as soon as Ron got back and spilled the truth, because the more she got to know Biff, the more she realized what an iron sense of propriety he had. That remark he had made at the Azure Room about people not teaching their kids table manners was only the tip of the iceberg. It seemed to her as if he was always telling her how important it was to keep your life on the straight and narrow, how you should carefully build a reputation so that people would know they could trust you, how you should work on controlling your impulses and be responsible and not indulge in alcohol. Sermons dropped from his lips constantly. It seemed obvious that under those formidable pectorals of his beat the heart of a steadfast Puritan. Odd to think that until the day she met him, she would have perfectly measured up to his exacting standards.

Her parents left with Susannah that afternoon as soon as her father got home from the store, and when it began getting dark, Ann-Marie backed the Mazda out of her driveway and headed in the direction of Felicia's. She was just driving down Elderberry Avenue when she realized a van was behind her. Casting a quick glance around the car, she was glad to see she had already locked all the doors. She could feel her heart thumping. She decided that no matter what happened, she would not stop the car.

Unfortunately, just at that moment, she came to a red light. A lifetime of being law-abiding was too much for her, and Ann-Marie found herself slowing to a stop. The van, however, did not stop. It kept going and bumped her car in the rear so that it quivered from the jolt. Startled, Ann-Marie looked around and saw that the hatchback had flown open. Through the open hatchback she could see two dark figures getting out of the van. She couldn't see them very clearly in the glare of the van's headlights, but suddenly she decided that if those men thought she was going to get out of her car to exchange insurance information they were in for a surprise. Without thinking twice, she stepped on the gas, running the red light. She could hear yells of protest behind her and there was a screech of brakes as a car heading toward her tried to avert a collision. She floored the accelerator, easily outdistancing the stopped van. Her heart was racing to keep pace with the car as she sped down Elderberry Road. There was no sign yet of the van in her rearview mirror. Nevertheless, afraid they might somehow catch up with her, she drove into the first full-service gas station she passed and pulled up in front of the attendant.

She rolled down the window. "Some men are following me," she panted. "Do you have a phone?"

"Sure thing," said the guy in the rumpled gray uniform. "I don't see anybody now, though."

Ann-Marie went inside and dialed Biff's number. His mother answered and Ann-Marie thought she sounded curious, but she didn't feel up to explaining her difficulties to a total stranger. "Biff?" she gasped, when he came to the phone. "Can you meet me at—" she glanced outside, "—the Amoco station on Elderberry and drive with me over to Felicia's? It's *not* my imagination. These guys in a van were following me and they bumped right into me. I don't think I'd better go on by myself."

"I'll be right there," said Biff.

As soon as he hung up, he pulled on his windbreaker and headed for the door.

"Where are you going, Biff?" his mother asked.

"Out," he said tersely.

"When do you think you'll be back?"

"Don't know," he said. He dashed out the front door and hopped in his car.

After he had left, his mother looked at his father meaningfully. "See there?" she said. "I told you so."

Biff was dimly aware that his parents didn't like him dashing off into the night after a mysterious phone call from a girl, but he had bigger worries. Two guys following Ann? What could be going on?

When he got to the Amoco station, Ann was standing by her car, hugging herself and shivering.

"Have you seen them since you got here?" he asked.

She shook her head. "But see where they hit me?"

Biff walked back with her to examine the car's bumper. There were a number of scrapes on the bumper, and it was hard to make out in the service station's light which were old scrapes and which new.

"And you see, the hatchback catch is broken. It's been temperamental for a while now. You really have to slam it to close it. I guess them bumping it was the coup de grace."

"What?"

"The final blow. They finished it off. You see, after they bumped me they got out of the car as if they were going to exchange insurance information with me, but I was afraid, so I just stepped on it and got out of there."

Biff ran his fingers along the bumper. "I think you did the right thing."

"Oh, Biff, I left the scene of an accident. That's a crime, isn't it?"

"Don't worry about it. It's not like you ran somebody down."

"But maybe I'd better call the police and report it," she said.

Biff looked uncomfortable. "Better not," he said. Until he figured out what was going on, he preferred for his dad's police pals not to be coming across Ann's name on an accident report. "It's just a little fender bender."

"And my parents!" Ann-Marie yelped. "I've wrecked the car!"

"Calm down, you haven't wrecked the car." He fingered the latch of the hatchback. "Look, bring it over to my house tomorrow and I'll patch it up for you. Your parents won't even have to know about it."

"Over to your place?" Ann-Marie asked. "Then I'll get to meet your parents."

"They're going to be in Durham all day," he said, with a trace of satisfaction. "Come on, let's go. I'll follow you over to Felicia's."

Chapter Eight

It turned out to be easy to fix the Mazda's latch. The loop of metal on the hatchback that caught in the latch had merely gotten bent and knocked out of alignment. A little careful work with a hammer and a screwdriver and the thing was fixed. Biff decided to finish the job up right by giving the car a thorough cleaning before he turned it over to Ann. If there was one thing he couldn't stand it was a junky car. The Twix wrappers, straws, sunflower seeds and spare change that littered the Mazda grated on him. He didn't know how Ann could stand it like that. He nourished the illusion that if people saw what a really clean car looked like, they would be willing to go to the trouble to keep it that way. He decided to show Ann how clean it could look.

He brought a wastebasket out to the car and began emptying the car of trash. It was amazing the things he got out of there—a comb, nail clippers, a felt marker, some red threads, several bits of the thin foil candy kisses are wrapped in. The car probably hadn't been cleaned out in months.

He picked up as much of it as he could, then connected up a heavy-duty extension cord to the vacuum cleaner. Of course, he thought, as he vacuumed the interior, you couldn't get as clean a look doing this as you could get if you kept the car up properly in the first place, but still he was sure Ann would notice the improvement. After he finished the interior, he dragged the vacuum around to the back and started trying to suck up the sand and sunflower seeds. The problem with vacuuming the hatchback was that over the sunken cubbyhole where the emergency spare tire was kept the lining was just a loose flap of carpeting, and if he wasn't careful the vacuum cleaner would suck the lining right up. Biff began by pushing the vacuum into the corners, flipping a few hard-to-reach sunflower seeds with his fingernail. That done, he began the final once-over. Even though he tried to go easy over the loose flap, sure enough the lining got sucked up by the vacuum and stuck there while the vacuum's sound changed to a protesting high-pitched whine. Biff cursed and began to try to pull the lining off the vacuum head.

As he bent over into the hatchback to do this, he noticed that something besides the spare tire was under the lining. It looked like a stiff, composition-board portfolio. Biff fished it out, wondering vaguely if it qualified as trash or what. He opened the thing up to peek inside and stunned, dropped the vacuum hose. The vacuum clattered against the car, then lay on the driveway sucking up bits of gravel with great rattling noises while Biff stared in silence at his grandfather's Rembrandt etchings.

Unbelievingly, he gently touched the edges of the etchings and felt the old rag paper. Then, aghast, he looked at his fingers to make sure they weren't dirty. Here he'd been cleaning a car and he'd gone and touched the etchings. He must be out of his mind. He was *clearly* out of his mind. He leaned on the car a minute, gripping the portfolio tightly and trying to collect his thoughts. The vacuum cleaner continued its high-pitched roar until finally he kicked its switch.

"What?" he said dazedly. He peeked inside the portfolio again and then closed it back up with a shudder. It all became clear now. Ron's intuition had been on target. Ann was mixed up with the Vinson boys and what she was mixed up in was the theft of his grandfather's etchings. It was unbelievable, but it was true.

Just then a horn blew and Felicia's car pulled up in front of the house. Ann bounced out of the car wearing a floppy beach hat and an oversize striped jacket over her swimsuit. Biff heard her thank Felicia for the ride, saw her walking toward him, her lips curved in a smile, her jacket opening slightly in the breeze to show the red swimsuit beneath. "It's fixed!" she said. "Oh, great." With a wave at them both, Felicia drove away.

"Do you recognize this?" Biff asked, lifting the portfolio.

"No," she said, looking puzzled. "It looks like an art portfolio. Was it in the car?"

Biff opened the portfolio and showed her the etchings inside. "What about these?" he said coldly.

She peered at them. "Why, aren't those some of Rembrandt's etchings? I remember some like that at the museum when our class went down to see the special exhibit." She reached for them. "Copies, I guess, huh?"

He stepped back, holding them out of reach. "No," he said. "Not copies. Originals. What were they doing in your car?"

"In my car? How could they be in my car?"

"That's what I was asking you," Biff said in an awful voice. "And I think I know the answer. You, Spike and Boomer stole them from my grandfather's house."

She blanched. "No! I don't know how they got there. Unless—gosh, it's just the kind of thing she would do. Je-rusalem! Ann B. must have stashed it there."

"What?"

"Ann Brierly," Ann-Marie said impatiently.

"So you admit it," he said.

"But *I'm* not Ann Brierly!" she exclaimed.

He took another step backward. "Oh? So who are you then?"

"Ann-Marie! I should have told you before, Biff, but I j-just couldn't. Ann B. and I are totally different. I mean, it's like night and day. I hate to think what she's up to. I expect I don't know the half of it. I thought she was gone and my troubles were over but now, you see, she's left me holding the bag. Ooo, I hate that girl."

"Look," Biff said, alarmed. "I can't handle this. I think you'd better take your car and get out of here." He threw the keys down to the gravel and, clutching the portfolio, ran toward the house. Behind him he could hear her calling, "Biff! Biff! Wait a minute! I can explain!"

When she rang the doorbell, a few minutes later, he didn't answer. He sat inside the empty house breathing heavily and wondering what to do next.

When Biff's parents and his sister got back from Durham late that afternoon, they found Biff sitting at the dining-room table reading. His mother bent sideways to read the spine of the book. "You're reading *The Three Faces of Eve*?" she asked, surprised.

"Yeah. I got it from the library. You know, this multiple-personality stuff is really scary."

"I guess so," his mother said.

"Did you know that one of the personalities can do something that the other personalities don't even know about? I mean like in this book, this woman would wake up and not know what she'd been doing for the past few days and it was all because the other personality had taken over." He ran his fingers through his hair. "This is really a serious personality disorder. I mean, big-time sick, we're talking."

"How did you suddenly get interested in psychiatry?" his dad asked, looking at him quizzically.

Biff flushed. "Oh, I don't know. You know how it is. Something catches your eye and then, well, you start reading it, that's all. Say, Dad, have you ever run into one of these multiple-personality types?''

"No, not as far as I know. I believe it's quite rare. What about you?''

"I don't know," Biff said slowly.

Jenny was pirouetting around the living room. "I'd make a wonderful split personality," she called. "Mrs. Grohman says I show great potential, that I could be anyone in life that I choose to be.''

"I don't think that's what she meant, Jenny," said her father.

The phone rang and Biff's mother picked it up. "Just a minute," Biff heard her say. "He's right here." She held out the phone to him. "It's for you, Biff.''

He jumped up. "I can't talk right now," he said. Grabbing his book, he headed back to his room. His mother cast a puzzled glance after him, shrugged and said into the receiver, "I'm sorry, he can't come to the phone right now. Can he return your call?''

After a moment, she looked up at her husband. "She hung up," she said.

"I wish I knew what was going on around here," he said. "I think it's time I had a talk with Biff.''

Biff's mother could hear him knocking on Biff's door and then Biff's muffled voice yelling, "Leave me alone. Can't a person have any peace around here, for Pete's sake? Go away."

Mr. Robertson didn't believe the lines of communication would be improved by his battering Biff's door down, so after a few minutes, he gave up.

Biff sat on his bed thinking hard. Could it be possible that Ann was a split personality? That sure would explain a lot. It would explain why the girl he knew seemed so different from the one he had heard Ron talking about. It was just like in that book he was reading—one of the personalities was very proper and another of them was a real wild type. The two of them didn't even like each other. "Like night and day," Ann had said. And maybe Ann didn't know about the etchings because the other personality had been the one that had stolen them.

Of course, it was hard to imagine someone you actually knew being a split personality, but he didn't think it was any harder than imagining the Ann he knew as a burglar.

Suddenly he remembered the guys who were following Ann in the van. They must have been trying to get to the etchings. Maybe it was Spike and Boomer who were following her. Maybe she had helped steal the etchings when she was in the personality she called "Ann B." and then forgot to give them over when she became this "Ann-

Marie." On the other hand, he had to consider
the possibility that she had only imagined that
these guys were following her. After all, she said
herself that the catch on the car had been acting
up for some time and he couldn't make out
whether those dents in the bumper had been
made last night or last year.

What a mess! Only one thing was clear in his
mind. He didn't want Ann to end up in jail for
grand larceny. For one thing, it looked to him
like she was a very sick girl. She needed help. For
another thing, he had to admit to himself that he
just didn't think he could stand it if she were sent
off to some reformatory or something with all
those tough types. His sweet little Ann—actually, when he thought about it, he felt more
sick to his stomach than anything.

But at least, what he was going to have to do
was clear enough. He had to make sure she got
some kind of help and he had to return the etchings to his grandfather.

"If you don't stop crying," Felicia said rea-
sonably into the telephone, "how can I possibly
understand what you're saying? Lighten up,
huh? It can't be the end of the world. Look,
maybe I'd better just come over."

A few minutes later, Felicia appeared at the door to Ann-Marie's house. "Golly," she said when the door was opened. "You look awful. You need some ice bags on those eyes. And what about some aspirin? I'll bet your sinuses are killing you after all that crying. Don't you think you'd better lie down?"

"Felicia!" Ann-Marie yelled. "Shut up!"

Undisturbed, Felicia perched on a cushion in the living room. "Your parents aren't back yet, huh?"

"They're staying over another night. They called."

"You'd better come over to my house, then, to spend the night."

Ann-Marie slumped on the couch. "Thank you but I prefer to sit here alone and drown in my misery." She sniffled. "It's worse than I even thought it would be, Felicia. He wouldn't believe me when I said I wasn't Ann B. He thinks I'm a criminal. He thinks I stole his grandfather's Rembrandt etchings. He won't even speak to me. He didn't even give me a chance to explain."

"His grandfather's Rembrandt etchings?"

"Well, I didn't mean I could explain *that*. I can't figure out how they got in my car."

"Let me get this straight. Biff found some Rembrandt etchings in your car."

"That's right. I think Ann B. must have hidden them in the back when she put her luggage back there. I remember thinking it was taking her an awful long time just to drop a few suitcases in the hatchback. Maybe there's some other explanation, but if there is, I can't figure out what it would be. Do you think Ann B. could have stolen those etchings?"

"Sure," said Felicia. "I can see her as a cat burglar, easy."

"Biff seemed to think she was in on it with Spike and Boomer."

"Well, there you go!" said Felicia. "You know two dodos like Spike and Boomer wouldn't have enough sense to steal a Rembrandt etching. They probably did the legwork and she had the idea."

"She must have thought of it when the whole class took that trip to the art museum," said Ann-Marie. "You remember how they had these little placards saying who had contributed each etching?"

"And they say education isn't broadening," said Felicia. "Well, look, you've just got to explain to him, that's all."

"How can I explain to him when he won't answer my phone calls, won't talk to me, won't believe what I say?" wailed Ann-Marie.

Felicia thought a minute. "It's tough," she admitted. "But maybe easier than explaining to the police, from whom you will be hearing shortly if you *don't* explain."

The doorbell rang and Ann-Marie turned white.

"You'd better answer it," suggested Felicia.

Ann-Marie tottered to the front door and flung it open. "Biff!" she exclaimed.

Felicia jumped up as if her chair had gotten an electric charge. "I'm out of here," she said brightly as she swept past Biff and made good her escape.

"Biff," cried Ann-Marie. "You've got to let me explain."

Biff closed the door behind him and took both her hands in his. "Look, Ann, I'm not going to stay long because to tell you the flat-out truth— I can't stand it. But I just wanted to tell you that you need to get help. You know, go talk to a psychiatrist."

"I am *not* crazy. If you would just listen to me—"

"Not crazy, exactly," said Biff in soothing tones, "but just a little confused. We could all stand to talk things over when we get a little confused.''

"I am *not* Ann Brierly," Ann-Marie said in dangerous tones. "Ann Brierly lives next door."

"Maybe you'd like to take me over and introduce me," Biff said pleasantly.

Ann-Marie looked momentarily confused. "Well, actually, she's not there now. She's at Disney World, you see. And her father is really sick, so I don't think I'd better—"

"That's what I thought," said Biff. "Look, I've got to go now. I just wanted to tell you that I'm going to do my best to keep my grandfather from telling the police what happened, but I can't guarantee anything. I want you to call a psychiatrist first thing Monday morning, okay? And I don't think we'd better talk to each other anymore until you start getting yourself straightened out."

"Biff!" she exclaimed, bunching her hands into fists in impotent fury.

But he had already turned and left. She staggered into the living room and fell onto the couch. "My driver's license!" she shrieked, pounding herself on the head. "Why didn't I show him my driver's license? I am so dumb! Dumb, dumb!"

But, she thought glumly, the way things were going he probably would just think she had stolen it.

Chapter Nine

Biff's grandfather picked up his favorite pipe off the desk in his study and began carefully stuffing it with tobacco from the humidor. "So what's all this hush-hush business about, Biff?" he asked, raising his eyebrows.

Biff fell into one of the old red-leather chairs, clutching the stiff portfolio to his chest. This was worse than a torn ligament. This was worse than losing the championship playoffs. His mouth was dry and he felt as if he had aged five years since yesterday.

"I've got something to tell you, that's all, sir," he said.

"Well, out with it! Something on your mind?"

Not able to find the right words, Biff opened the portfolio and very carefully placed "Angels Appearing to the Shepherds" on top of the stiff fiberboard.

His grandfather leaned over to peer at the paper and recognizing it at once, sucked in his breath sharply. With a shaking hand he reached behind him to replace the pipe on the desk.

"Are you trying to tell me you took them?" his grandfather said harshly.

"Good Lord, no, sir! I just happened to find them."

"You just happened to *find* them?" his grandfather choked. "Listen, Biff, I'd rather I never saw those wretched things again, I'd prefer to shred them and stuff them in my pipe and burn them both, I say, than to think you had any part whatsoever in this affair."

"I didn't! I didn't know anything about it! I was just telling you that I found them."

"You found them."

"Right."

"Want to tell me about it?"

"Well, yesterday," Biff began hesitantly, "I found them in somebody's car."

"Whose car?"

Biff squirmed. "I'd rather not say, sir. The thing is, I sort of think this person is not really responsible and she *is* going to get help. If it's okay with you I'd rather leave it at that."

"This person is a woman?"

"Well, yeah. Sort of."

"Don't be absurd, Biff," barked his grandfather. "Someone either is a woman or is not. There's no such thing as 'sort of a woman.' Why don't you say what you mean?"

"A girl, I mean."

"This girl is someone you are involved with," his grandfather said heavily.

"Sort of." Catching a look at his grandfather he added hastily, "What I mean is I used to go out with her, but not anymore. I mean, I'm certainly not going to go out with her anymore. After this, I mean."

"Do your parents know about this girl?"

"Not exactly."

"I thought not. Biff, let me tell you, when a man is young, he may imagine that he is learning something of life by hanging around low dives, drinking, gambling and fraternizing with women of ill repute, but let me assure you that is the path to destruction."

Biff looked at his grandfather, aghast. He had heard his father joke about his grandfather's famous speeches from the bench that left hardened criminals with tears in their eyes, but had never imagined that he would be on the receiving end of one.

"Think of your sainted mother and all the sacrifices she has made for you," his grandfather said huskily. "Think of your dear father, who has his faults, I don't deny, but who has loved you from the moment you were born. Your father would walk through fire for you, Biff. And what should be your return for all that love that has surrounded you since the day you were born, your return for all those sacrifices of your sainted mother? When you start to step into one of those dives, when you are tempted by one of those women, think of them."

"It's not like that, sir," Biff said weakly, but his grandfather did not seem to hear him.

Taking the portfolio from Biff, he placed it on his desk. Standing stiffly, he stared at "Angels Appearing to the Shepherds" a moment. Then he turned back to glare at Biff.

"So what am I going to tell the insurance company, Biff? What am I going to tell the police? Have you given any thought to that?"

"I don't know, sir. But I'm asking you not to tell the police anything about it." Biff looked right into his grandfather's eyes. "In fact, sir, I'm begging you."

"You didn't have anything to do with it?"

"I give you my word," Biff said stiffly.

There was a moment of silence. Finally his grandfather spoke. "I'll think about it," he said.

Biff rose from the chair.

"You promise me you didn't know anything about it?" his grandfather repeated sharply.

"Yes!" Biff cried. "I just told you. How could I have known anything about it? I was just as surprised as you are."

Reaching for the doorknob, he thought of how satisfying it would be to strangle Ann.

"Biff?" said his grandfather.

Biff's hand rested on the doorknob as he looked behind him.

"I haven't claimed yet on the insurance," his grandfather said.

Biff pulled the door open and fled.

"Biff, darling, do you have to rush off?" said his grandmother. "I'm just about to take cookies out of the oven."

Biff, in a headlong course to get out of the house as soon as possible, stopped suddenly. "Gram, you know I wouldn't do anything to hurt you and Granddad, don't you?"

"Why, of course, darling," she said in a bewildered voice. "What's going on, Biff?"

"Nothing. I've, uh, got to run," he said. What had he ever done to deserve all this? he asked himself as he dashed out to his car.

As he drove home, he found himself feeling mildly hopeful that Grandfather would drop the idea of tracking down the culprit. The remark about the insurance, he suspected, had been his grandfather's way of telling him he would be able to let the matter drop. Biff didn't like to think about it, but he supposed that if his grandfather imagined he was hanging around in low dives picking up women, that might be another reason he would prefer not to pursue the investigation. He wouldn't want the scandal that would result if Biff's connection to the thief were exposed. He only hoped his grandfather didn't feel duty bound to tell the whole story to his father.

Of course, everyone was bound to wonder how the etchings had been recovered, but Biff knew no one would dare question his grandfather if he indicated the matter wasn't up for discussion. He supposed the police and everyone else would just assume his grandfather had made a private deal with the thieves to ransom the etchings.

Biff could feel his anger toward Ann fading. All he felt now was sadness and a deep sense of exhaustion. Whenever he thought of Ann, he felt like crying.

When he arrived back at his house he spotted a red Camaro parked out front and his heart sank. With everything else he had on his mind, he had forgotten that this was the day Ron was due back. Great. Ron in a homicidal mood. Just what he needed right now.

As soon as Biff went in the side door, his mother looked up from the bunch of zinnias she was arranging and said, "Ron's in your room waiting for you, Biff. He seemed to be awfully anxious to see you."

"Yeah," Biff muttered.

"Biff? Is everything okay?"

Biff managed a wobbly smile. "Sure, Mom. Hey, what could be wrong?"

As he mounted the steps, he carefully took his hands out of his pockets so they would be free if he needed to fend Ron off. When he reached his room, he opened his door very slowly, standing back a little as he did so.

Then he saw Ron sitting in the swivel chair at the desk. He turned around to face Biff as he came in. Biff noticed that Ron had acquired a deep tan and that his teeth were flashing in a smile, but it was a gunslinger's sort of smile—mean.

"Biff, old buddy," Ron said.

"Hi, there, Ron." Biff shut the door behind him.

Ron leaned toward him ominously and lowered his voice. "I'd just like you to name some place where I could rip your face off, old buddy."

"Look, Ron, it's not the way you think."

"How do you know what I think, you reptile, you double-crossing, pitiful excuse for a friend." Ron's eyes were narrow, angry slits, but Biff hardly noticed. Here, at last, he suddenly realized with a sense of relief, was somebody he could talk to about Ann.

"Look, Ron, I finally found out what Ann was up to with Spike and Boomer. You were right. The three of them must have been in on it together. They stole my grandfather's Rembrandt etchings."

Ron blanched. "Your grandfather's Rembrandt etchings? My God, that's grand larceny! They sucked her into it. I just know it. That's just the kind of thing I was afraid of."

"I found the etchings in her car. I think maybe Spike and Boomer had been trying to get at them for days but she always kept the car locked up in her garage. Naturally she denied it all."

Ron's brow was furrowed. "Maybe she didn't know she had the etchings," he suggested. "Maybe Spike and Boomer just stashed them in her car. When you think about it, there could be a perfectly logical explanation for this, Biff."

"Sure, there could," Biff said heavily. "Tell me this, Ron, has it ever occurred to you that Ann might have a split personality?"

Ron looked at him incredulously for a moment, then laughed. "A joke, huh? A sick joke. Heck, no, Ann doesn't have a split personality. The one she's got is headache enough. Which reminds me—"

"I'm not kidding, Ron. Now listen to me. The Ann I got to know just seemed like a totally different kind of person from the girl you told me about."

"Well, naturally, different people see things—"

"The Ann I got to know was a sort of shy type, delicate, you know, like a fawn."

Ron looked at him in surprise for a moment, then chortled. "She was putting you on, Biff old boy. I get it now. She didn't like it when she found out I asked you to keep an eye on her. She pulled all this shy stuff just to string you along. Yeah, now that I think of it, this stuff of pretending to fall for you, that was all part of the joke. She was getting back at me for getting somebody to check up on her. That's what must have happened."

"She wasn't pretending, Ron."

"Sure, sure. You took it hook, line and sinker, that's all. Ann's not your type. I saw that right from the start. She's a party girl. She loves to kick up a dust, cause a commotion, be right there at the center of things."

"She reads all the time," Biff said. "She likes poetry."

"Likes poetry? That's a laugh. Ann's idea of great literature is her collection of Garbage Pail Kids cards. Golly, I'm sorry now that I missed the whole thing," Ron said, leaning back in the chair with a grin. "Ann pretending to like poetry. You eating it all up. It must have been a stitch."

"Don't you see there could be two Anns?" Biff asked. "Listen, when I let her know I had caught her with those Rembrandt etchings and that the game was up, she started saying she wasn't Ann Brierly, that she was somebody called Ann-Marie. Ann Brierly, she said, did all the bad things and Ann-Marie was the good one. Don't you see? It's a classic case of a split personality."

Ron was wiping tears of laughter out of his eyes. "I never should have let her get at you, Biff. You were like catnip to her, an innocent type like you. I can't believe you bought all that stuff. She's probably laughing her head off right now, no kidding."

Biff scarcely knew which affronted him more, being called innocent or being called a fool. "She is not laughing," he said in a dangerous tone. "And neither am I."

"I know it's hard to admit somebody played you for a sucker, Biff. I understand that." Ron burst into laughter again. He shook his head. "I just hope she's still speaking to me, that's all. Well, I'll have to tell her that she got her revenge, all right. I really was worried there. I thought she really had fallen for you."

"She has."

"Aw, come on, now. I just told you how it was a joke."

"Well, why don't we just go ask her?"

Ron stared at him in astonishment. "Well, okay. But don't you think you're going to feel pretty silly?"

"No, I don't. Do you think I'm so out of it I can't tell if a girl really likes me, for Pete's sake. You must really think I'm some kind of idiot."

"Well, okay, if you insist, *idiot*, we'll call her up right now."

"She's not at home. She was supposed to do the face-painting booth at the Fun Fair this afternoon."

"So, we'll go right over to the Fun Fair," Ron said loudly.

"Okay," Biff almost shouted. "Okay, we'll just do that."

As the two boys thundered downstairs and headed for the front door, Biff called out, "Mom! We're going over to the Fun Fair."

She looked after them dubiously as they charged out, slamming the door behind them. "Well, boys, have—" she hesitated "—fun," she concluded lamely.

Chapter Ten

Biff's car skidded up to the parking lot behind Sunset Park just after Ron's Camaro. The two friends, silently furious, got out of their cars, stomped across the street and began making their way with determination past the strolling groups of people attending the fair.

Just past the miniature golf course, the boys ran into a trio of seventh-grade girls whose faces were boldly painted in hearts and flowers. One had a blue nose, set off by some blue initials on one cheek. Another's cheek proclaimed in green letters I Love Roger. All three girls wore identical floppy hats and were licking identical strawberry ice-cream cones.

"Where did you get that done?" Biff demanded.

Confronted by such a huge and intimidating older boy, the girls' mouths fell open in dismay and they were struck speechless.

"The face painting," Biff said impatiently. "Where did you have all that face painting done?"

One of the girls finally gathered together enough courage to turn and point in the direction of the baseball diamond.

"Thanks," said Biff. He and Ron charged along the sidewalk, sidestepping crying toddlers and a number of families that seemed to have never heard of population control. All around them, fairgoers dressed in shorts and halters were devouring sticky and drippy foods—cotton candy, hot dogs with chili sauce, caramel popcorn.

"Good grief," said Ron. "Everybody and his brother is out here."

A band of brass instruments added its strident sounds to the tinkly oompah-oompah of the merry-go-round.

"Mom-my!" wailed a little child.

"I told you you shouldn't let him eat all that junk," said a resigned male voice. "Now I'll bet he's going to throw up."

"What a zoo!" Ron exclaimed. "Hey, there she is!"

"I see her!" Biff cried. "Right over there next to the hot dog booth."

The band was so loud now the boys had to shout to be heard. "No, not by the hot dog booth," yelled Ron. "Over there in the balloon. See?"

Ron waved his arm. The girl in the basket of the balloon stopped licking her giant sucker long enough to smile and wave back. Biff could see that she was wearing what looked like black felt Mickey Mouse ears.

"Hey, that's not my Ann," he protested indignantly.

"Well, it's *my* Ann," said Ron. He began running over to the balloon.

"Hurry up, Ronnie," the girl in the Mickey Mouse ears shrieked. "We're going to blast off!"

Biff watched in bewilderment as he saw Ron loping across the baseball diamond. Once he reached the balloon, he clambered his way up in its basket and threw his arms around the girl in the mouse ears. Ron and the girl were still kissing when Biff turned his eyes back to the face-painting booth where Ann sat. She did not seem to have seen him. She was sitting with her arms resting on the edge of the booth, her hands buried in her hair in a gesture of despair that reminded him of the first time he had seen her.

He walked over to the booth and stood squarely in front of her.

"Hi," he said.

Her eyes rose swiftly to his face. "Biff!" she cried.

"So you aren't Ron's Ann, huh?"

"That's what I've been trying to tell you!"

"So who are you?" he asked hoarsely.

"Ann-Marie Echersley. I live next door to Ann B. We're in the same class at school. When she stole some of my clothes, she left one of her T-shirts behind, you see," she said quickly. "That's why I was wearing her T-shirt. And then I took her to the train station when she went to Disney World. I think she stashed the etchings in my car then, do you see?"

"No, I don't see. I don't see at all. Why did you tell me you were Ron's girl?"

"Because you were *looking* for Ron's girl," she said. "Don't you see? I knew you would never notice me if I were just plain old Ann-Marie. You'd just move on and I'd never see you again. You do understand, don't you, Biff?"

"When I think how I worried about you," he said thickly. "When I think how I went to my grandfather and *begged* him not to turn you into the cops. Right this minute," he went on in a shaking voice, "my grandfather is over there thinking that I pick up sleazy women in bars. And all because I was trying to *protect* you. What a laugh. I'm the one that needed protection from you. And another thing—what about all those nights I worried myself sick about double-crossing Ron? And you said you liked me? Ha. My worst enemy wouldn't have put me through all that." He took a deep breath. "Well, at least it's over. I never have to see you again. And that is going to be a pleasure, I can tell you." He took his hands out of his pockets, suddenly aware of an overpowering urge to wreck the face-painting booth. It would be great to up-end the whole flimsy structure and jump up and down on the fragments. He looked at his hands incredulously a minute and then muttered, "I'd better get out of here before I do something I'll be sorry for."

Ann-Marie scarcely saw him walk away through the blur of tears that filled her eyes.

A minute later she heard Felicia's voice. "Not one of your better days, I gather," she commented.

"Oh, Felicia," Ann-Marie sobbed. "He hates me."

"Oh, well, look on the bright side."

"*What* bright side?" wailed Ann-Marie, knocking over the blue paint in her efforts to get at a handkerchief.

Felicia looked at her sympathetically. "Come on," she said. "I'd better drive you home."

As soon as Ann-Marie got home, she ran to her room and threw herself on the bed.

"Go ahead and cry," said Felicia. "You'll feel better."

"Dough I won't," Ann-Marie sobbed, lifting her head. "I'll feel worse. My head will ache and I'll feel even more awful, if that is humanly possible."

Mrs. Echersley's brown head poked in the door. "Is anything wrong, girls?" she asked.

"No," sobbed Ann-Marie. "Everything's just fine." She buried her face in her pillow.

After Felicia left, Ann-Marie told her mother the whole story.

"Well," her mother said gently, "we all make mistakes. We just have to learn from them, don't we?"

"I don't want to learn from my mistakes," sniffed Ann-Marie. "I want Biff back."

"There is no calamity greater than lavish desires," her mother murmured.

"What?"

"That's what the sage Lao-tzu said."

"Oh, Mother! Please, *don't* go all hippie on me now," sobbed Ann-Marie.

That night, Biff couldn't sleep. He finally got out of bed at 1:00 a.m., went into the kitchen, switched on the light and poured himself a glass of milk. The milk looked kind of lonely sitting by itself on the table, so he opened the refrigerator and began rummaging around. He tossed out a package of salami, some Swiss cheese and a bag of lettuce. Then he pulled out two kinds of mustard and a large jar of kosher dill pickles. "Rye," he muttered. "Wonder where it is?" He began flinging open cupboard doors looking for the rye bread.

The kitchen door opened and Biff's mother came in yawning, wrapped in her husband's old burgundy bathrobe. "I thought I heard somebody get up," she said.

Biff pulled the bread down from the cupboard and began swabbing mustard onto it. His mother glanced at him, then began rattling around in the pots in the bottom cupboard. A moment later she produced a small pot.

"Want some cocoa?" she asked. "I'm fixing some for myself."

"No, thanks," said Biff. "I'll just have milk."

He began stacking slices of salami, Swiss cheese and pickle on the bread.

His mother took a deep breath. "Is something on your mind, Biff? Do you want to talk?"

He precariously balanced the final slice of rye on top of his huge concoction. "I was just thinking I might give Cynthia a call," he said.

Her eyes opened wide. "At one o'clock in the morning?"

"No. Not now. Later."

"Oh."

He took a large bite of his sandwich. This disturbance to the delicate structure of the sandwich sent several bits of lettuce and a pickle tumbling to the table, but he didn't seem to notice. "The thing is," he said, his voice somewhat muffled because his mouth was full, "with Cynthia you know where you are." He chewed thoughtfully for a moment, then added, "She really understands soccer, too."

Biff's mother regarded his broad back with hopelessness. Boys are so much harder to raise than girls, she thought, I don't care what anybody says.

Saturday night, Biff was at a drive-in movie with Cynthia. A mosquito buzzed past his ear in the darkness. He slapped at it and hit his nose instead. He was beginning to think the drive-in had been a mistake. When he had decided on it, he'd been looking for a place he'd be sure not to run into Ann-Marie. He had forgotten about the heat, the mosquitoes and the generally run-down air of the place. This drive-in, the only one in town, specialized in skin flicks and horror shows. Biff noticed that only four cars had turned out tonight to see *Sorority Chain Saw Massacre*.

Cynthia's strong white teeth crunched on her buttered popcorn. Her eyes were fixed on the buxom sorority sister on screen who was beginning to undress. Biff glanced briefly at the screen. That bimbo's got a life expectancy of about ten seconds, he thought. More disturbing to him than the sorority sister's imminent demise was that he could see Cynthia was spilling a few kernels of popcorn every time she reached in the box. Biff hated the way popcorn kernels got wedged down between the seat cushions. And on top of that, there was the little matter of the grease spots on the upholstery. On screen, just as the sorority girl opened her mouth wide to scream there was a crackling and whirring noise and the frames began spinning past, crooked. Then the screen went white.

"Golly!" Cynthia exclaimed, twisting around to look back at the projection booth. "What happened?"

"Looks like the filmstrip broke," said Biff.

"We are experiencing temporary technical difficulties," said a voice over the speaker. "Would you please stand by?"

"Forget it," Biff said in disgust. "What do you say we scratch the movie and go get a hamburger?"

"Okay," said Cynthia.

At least, thought Biff with resignation, she's finished the popcorn.

As they slowly drove out of the darkened lot, Cynthia thrust her fist against her left hand and absentmindedly began cracking her knuckles.

Ann-Marie found that as the summer wore on, she needed more and more time to herself to think. She began packing a lunch to take over to City Lake. City Lake was a bit of nature the town of Farmingdale had preserved in the midst of its suburban sprawl. On one side the lake was bordered by one of the busiest thoroughfares in Farmingdale, but a park wound around the rest of it. It was a favorite place for mothers with small children to come feed the ducks or for office workers to drive over to for a quick bag lunch under a tree. At this time of year, thirteen American flags fluttered in the breeze, left there after the Fourth of July celebration, their stars and stripes reflected in the lake during the moments when it was unruffled by breezes.

Ann-Marie always took a book with her when she went to the lake. Sitting on a bench under a tree with a book and a sandwich, she could look up now and then to watch the squabbling of the ducks over the bits of bread children threw for them. She liked being near the water when she was thinking peaceful thoughts of the sort that preoccupied her lately—thoughts about the endless passing of time, the crumbling of great empires, the futility of all human ambition. Deep thoughts.

Today she had brought a volume of W. H. Auden's poetry. She loved Auden's poetry because it was so full of irony.

> Lay your sleeping head, my love
> Human on my faithless arm

That said it all. Life was full of imperfections. Disappointment was what you had to learn to expect.

Once her command of French was a little more secure, say, after college sometime, Ann-Marie decided she would definitely move to Paris and would earn her bread by writing bitter, insightful poetry that would be dripping with irony. If she should run into Biff, which was, to be sure, quite unlikely in Paris, she would not be thrown off balance a bit. Mature and sophisticated, she would give him a wise smile, lift her eyebrow ironically and let him know that what had happened between them was all so long ago, so far away, that it no longer caused her pain. Maybe they would have lunch together, even. Unless, that is, he was still mad.

Ann-Marie was so intent on her thoughts that she didn't notice Biff's car when it drove up. He parked about twenty-five yards from her, got out and looked in her direction. He took a step toward her, then hesitated, stuck his hands in his pockets and stared out at the water. After he had stood there a moment, he suddenly turned and began walking toward Ann-Marie. A bit later, she heard a twig crack and looked up, startled.

"Biff!" she said faintly. She had forgotten how big he was. The sun fell on his blue knit shirt, dappling it. Under the tree, with the breeze ruffling his hair a little, he seemed as much a part of the out-of-doors as the trees and the ducks.

Abruptly he sat down next to her. "Hi," he said. He did not look at her but stared out at the lake. Not far from them, a four-year-old, one hand held tightly by his mother, was throwing bread to the ducks. A goose grabbed a choice piece of this largesse and sped quickly out of reach of his quacking pursuers.

"What are you doing these days?" Ann-Marie asked.

"Nothing much," he said. "What about you?"

"The same," she said. "Nothing in particular. I'm working mornings now, in my father's store."

"What does he do?" Biff asked with a crooked smile.

"He has a health food store."

"Figures," he said gloomily.

"Biff, I'm really sorry—"

"I don't want to talk about it," he said.

"Well, then what did you come over here for?" Ann-Marie said with some indignation.

He thought about it a minute. "I guess I wanted to see you," he said.

She impulsively reached for his hand. To her relief he didn't pull it away, and they sat for a while holding hands and watching the ducks.

"I save my crust for the ducks," she said. "Do you want to help me throw it?"

"Sure," he said. She dumped a handful of crusts into his palm and the two of them stood with their shoes practically in the grassy mud, throwing the bits out into the water. The ducks, however, were not particularly interested in a few bread crusts, having eaten their fill from the loaf thrown out by the four-year-old.

Ann-Marie shot a nervous glance at Biff as she threw out her last crumb. "Are you the kind of person who stays mad a long time?" she asked.

"Sort of," he admitted.

"I was just thinking about how when I'm out of college, I'm going to go live in Paris," she said breathlessly, "and if you come over to Paris anytime, maybe we could have lunch together."

"I don't think I'm going to stay mad that long," he said.

Ann-Marie took a deep breath. "Good," she said.

He put his arm around her and squeezed her close to his side. "I'm not nearly as mad as I was."

She smiled at him. "Good."

"Maybe we could have lunch tomorrow, even, and not wait till you move away to Paris."

She leaned her face against his arm and said in a muffled voice, "I'd like that. I'd really like it."

"Me, too," he said, smiling foolishly at the top of her head.

*   *   *   *   *

I heard a mellow voice behind my left shoulder. "Pardon me, but aren't you the candidate's daughter? The one who just spoke?"

"Guilty," I said, turning around to view an amazingly handsome face checking me out with melting brown eyes. Though I was too startled to take in the details, I got a general impression of tasteful elegance. A sweater of subdued color and well-creased slacks.

He put out his hand and grasped mine. "I'm Sterling Huffaker," he said. "I've been admiring you from afar. What a break for me that I had an errand in the bookstore, and got a chance to meet you in person, away from the crowds."

It was beyond belief that such a guy would be treating me like a celebrity. He kept his eyes on me with an expression of awe, and I knew how stars must feel when confronted by their fans....

**How do you break up with a sweet guy like Ernie?
As Amy soon finds out,**

IT ISN'T EASY!

For a good laugh, read

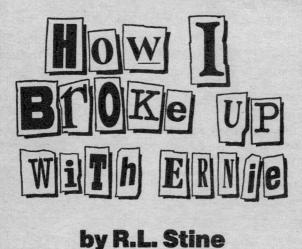

by R.L. Stine

Available from Crosswinds in September

COMING NEXT MONTH
FROM
Keepsake

KEEPSAKE # 31
FOREIGN EXCHANGE
by Brenda Cole

For years Lorrie had idolized Sam Young. Now she had a chance to get his attention. Would he live up to her dreams?

KEEPSAKE # 32
THE GANG'S ALL HERE
by Janice Harrell

The first book in a fun new miniseries starring the kids in The In Crowd.

AVAILABLE THIS MONTH

KEEPSAKE # 29
MASQUERADE
Janice Harrell

KEEPSAKE # 30
SPRING BREAK
Bebe Faas Rice

Blushing Beauty—Do's and Don'ts

Avoid colors that are very different from your natural cheek color.

A defined line looks unnatural. Blend your rouge well so no one can see where color begins or ends.

Don't blush in a strip so wide that it covers your entire face. Blush is used to highlight cheekbones and add color to the face. Don't overdo.

Never apply blusher too close to the center of your face. Feel your face. Notice that the prominent part of your cheekbone starts around the area under the center of your eye, not at the bridge of your nose.

Practice with gels. A little squirt goes a long way.

Applying blush without a mirror is a mistake. Always watch what you're doing.

Don't apply blush before foundation. If you're wearing foundation, apply it first, blush second.

If you've tried applying a little blush as directed above but feel that you'd like to make a little more (or less) of your face shape, there are a few contouring tricks you can try with cheek color. Be sure to play and practice at home to see what works best for you. A few afternoons in front of the mirror will make you a makeup pro!

1. Think about the shape of your face. Is it square? Round? Rectangular? Triangular? Oval?

2. A hint for the round face: Put a dot of color on your chin and blend it in. This will help lengthen your face a bit.

3. Is your face long and narrow, like a rectangle? To soften the hard lines and widen your face, concentrate blush on the outer edges of your face. This will draw attention away from the length and give more width where you need it.

4. To minimize the hard lines of a square face, apply blusher normally, then dot a bit of extra color on your chin and the middle of your forehead. Blend well.

5. Triangular or heart-shaped face? Avoid putting blusher on your chin. It will only call attention to it.

6. Oval face? Anything goes. Try a hint of blush on earlobes, too, to give a fresh, country look—as if you've just come in from the great outdoors.

═══ CROSSWINDS™

TELEPHONE OFFER
ONE PROOF OF PURCHASE

✂ **August 1988**

Limited Quantities Available

ORDER FORM

Name _____

Street Address _____ Apt. # _____

City _____ State _____ ZIP _____

Orders must be postmarked no later than October 31, 1988. Incomplete orders will not be honored.

Send your check or money order for $5.00 with two proofs of purchase (one July, one August) and this order form to:

CROSSWINDS TELEPHONE OFFER
901 Fuhrmann Blvd.
P.O. Box 1396
Buffalo, N.Y. 14240-9954
U.S.A.

OFFER NOT VALID IN AUSTRALIA

POP-TEL-1UR